Terror on Sunshine Boulevard

By J.Q. Rose

Amazon Print ISBN 978-0-2286-0925-4

BWL Publishing Inc.

Books we love to write ...
Authors around the world.

http://bwlpublishing.ca

Dedication

This book is dedicated to all the first responders who are always ready to come to our aid in any emergency.

Chapter One

Gloria Hart burst through the double glass doors of the large multi-purpose room of their park's community center. She was delighted to see all of the ladies still standing in groups around the large room instead of poised to begin the exercise class. She was running late. Although a resident of Citrus Ridge Senior Community for more than three years, she'd driven along Sunshine Boulevard, the main artery around the park, and missed the turn-off to the community center.

Gloria re-shouldered her heavy bag holding her water bottle and barbells, and moved her rolled exercise mat under her arm to keep it from crushing against her chest. She dropped her bag on the floor and unrolled the mat in the spot she always claimed at every class meeting. Like pew seats in a Sunday morning church service, each person staked out her favorite "place" to exercise and kept it.

She hustled over to join the big circle of friends in their usual space in the room. The ladies shifted a bit to make space for Gloria in the circle. She breathed a sigh of relief knowing she wasn't late again. Being late was a sign of disrespect, but Gloria respected every gal in this room for exercising their bodies and joining in the group. Perhaps they didn't all do the moves like their limber instructor, Bridgett, but at least they tried.

Gloria noted several circles of women around the room. A flashback to eighth grade when her clique of classmates stood in the hall before class. Memories danced through her mind of best friends, gossip, and popularity contests. Odd how things were still the same nearly fifty years later.

"Good morning, everyone." She smiled widely as she greeted her friends. But instead of the usual happy chorus of "Good morning Gloria," her friends in the circle weakly smiled with the acknowledgement of her presence. Silence fell over the group. Everyone's eyes lasered in on her. Gloria felt uncomfortable. What were they waiting for?

Finally her friend Pamela asked, "Well, are you going to tell us about George McDonnell?" Her voice a higher pitch. "Did Jim hear anything yet?" Pamela's voice ratcheted even higher.

Gloria turned to face Pamela. "No, I haven't heard anything. Why? Is he sick?"

"No, he's dead." Rosemary, Pamela's best friend, waited a beat for Gloria to absorb the news. "Jim's one of the first responders for the park. Wasn't he called to the scene yesterday?"

"Uh, no. We were gone all day." The unexpected news slammed her like a wild pickle ball, nearly knocking her off her feet and stinging her heart. George was younger than she was for Pete's sake. He couldn't be dead. That was incomprehensible to her. She and her husband had just visited him last week. He was a healthy man for his age. Tears stung her eyes when she remembered how excited he was about a fishing trip he'd planned.

Pamela gave her an understanding smile, flashing her perfect teeth—all her own—and touched Gloria's back.

Gloria studied each woman's face, hoping one of them would explain further while her mind tried to process the news. Many of the residents in the senior community mistakenly assumed Jim attended every call because he was the volunteer co-captain of the First Responders Unit, but Jim wasn't on-call yesterday. She hadn't heard the latest happenings in the park because they'd shopped most of the day at the flea market and relished a delicious fish dinner at their favorite restaurant, Magoo's, arriving there just in time to get in on the early bird specials.

A flash of guilt surged through her mind. Should she and Jim have checked on George? Maybe they could have saved him if they had stopped by his house before they'd left for the day.

"I can hardly believe George is dead. I had no idea he had heart problems. He seemed to be the picture of health," Gloria said.

"Oh, no. Nobody knows yet if it was his heart or what killed him," Bonnie, another woman in the group, announced.

Gloria was puzzled as she saw the looks of horror exchanged by her friends.

"What happened?" Her eyes widened with concern, and then realized she had been drawn into the gossip like everyone else.

Bonnie puffed up her chest and pulled her elbows back as she leaned forward to deliver the big news. "His neighbor, Lottie Carpenter found him. She *smelled* him rotting in his house." She wrinkled her nose in disgust.

"Oh, my word." Gloria covered her mouth and wanted to gag as if she smelled poor George. "That poor man. I cannot imagine…"

At the front of the room, Bridgett clapped her hands to get the ladies' attention. "Okay, everyone, are we ready to get moving this morning?"

With that announcement, the circles of women broke up and the ladies rushed to their mats. Gloria's questions wouldn't be answered now, but the exercises could help her avoid thinking of George dying alone in his house. And rotting? She shook her head and squinched her eyes to try and erase the picture in her mind of their dead friend.

Gloria was disappointed in herself being drawn into the gossip. The twice-a-week gatherings to catch up with friends at the class were highlights in Gloria's week, but she hated the spreading of gossip by several individuals.

She enjoyed sharing information about places to see and where to eat a good meal for not a lot of money, catching up on their families and friends, even exchanging recipes. Stretching her muscles was another plus.

Gloria grabbed the barbells out of her bag and placed them by her mat. With a quick prayer that the instructor wouldn't use them today, she began stretching and moving and joining the thirty-two women marching in place as the instructor led them in arm circles.

The women were all senior citizens but each one had her own way of expressing herself with her exercise outfits. Some wore t-shirts and old shorts, others in yoga pants and classy shirts which absorbed the "moisture", while others looked like advertisements for the company who sold the high-style wear.

Gloria glanced at Pamela standing next to her. Pamela had removed her jacket revealing a slim, tanned figure. As usual she had applied her makeup to her beautiful face and she glowed. Today she wore a matching pink tank top which outlined her perky bosom, tight pink shorts and coordinating tennis shoes and socks. Gloria felt a little dumpy next to her in her free navy blue t-shirt she'd received from the lumber company and her capris with the stretched waist band. But she was comfortable and easily moved unencumbered by those tight yoga pants worn by so many of the ladies.

At her age, Gloria thought she was done with role models, but she admired Pamela as if she were the head of her junior high school clique. Not only was Pamela beautiful, but she was also gracious and self-confident, friendly and kind. Gloria wanted to be just like her even if she were a senior citizen now and not a teen.

After a few minutes, they stopped to practice cleansing breaths. Next, Bridgett counted off the shoulder rolls, five with the left, then five with the right, and finally both arms at the same time.

Gloria messed up which shoulder to raise when she thought of George and wondered if Jim had been notified yet. Stretching her sides and back with the group, she tried to focus on the movements and counting how many times she alternately touched her toes.

Concentrating on exercising was difficult with all the questions about George's death swirling through her head. The group of ladies talking and giggling as they exercised near her also ruined her concentration.

Then she heard the tooting on the other side of her. The undeniable, no-way-to-cover-it loud explosions of gas! Somehow all this movement got the body, as well as the gas inside, moving. Little bubbles and big ones escaped without any warning. Most of the time the women never said anything, but today the sound was loud enough for the whole group to hear the resounding bombs. Finally all the ladies broke out in laughter that rolled throughout the room.

Gloria was glad for the interruption. The giggling helped to clear her thoughts of sadness about George's death for a few minutes, but couldn't erase them completely.

"Now, ladies, pick up your weights." All of the women grabbed their barbells, except Gloria. Instead, she shoved her weights back into her bag. She had to get home to tell Jim about George's death. Or perhaps by now, he would have heard about it and could explain what killed George.

Pamela side-stepped over to her while lifting her barbells up to her shoulders. "Everything okay?"

"It's George." Gloria's throat closed, leaving her unable to speak. She stooped over and rolled her mat up on the floor.

"Sorry, I have to go. I'll talk to you later." Gloria didn't give her a chance to reply or ask questions as she rushed for the door and out into the parking lot.

She didn't even notice the warmth of the winter sunlight on her face when she exited the peach colored Spanish-style Community Center. The regal palms against the blue sky outlined the parking lot on the fringes of the bocce ball, shuffleboard and pickle ball courts.

Gloria pitched her bag in the back seat, slammed the back door of the Buick, then settled in the driver's seat. She took a deep breath to calm herself before turning on the ignition. Always a careful driver, she checked the rear-view mirror to see if a walker or bicycler was behind her, then backed the car out of the parking spot and maneuvered through the lot passing the swimming pool and golf clubhouse complex.

Looking right, then left, and spotting no golf carts or vehicles on the road, she turned onto the street leading to Sunshine Boulevard. She usually relished driving along the four lane road that circled the outer perimeter of the double-wide homes in the large park. Lush plantings of palm trees, native Florida plants, and seasonal flowers growing in dense beds enhanced the median separating the lanes. Moisture collected in her eyes as she breathed in the beauty of the scene knowing George would never experience a beautiful day like this again.

As soon as she turned onto her street, Lemon Avenue, she smashed her foot on the brake to avoid running over Mr. Tweeble. Sitting comfortably in his red electric four-wheeled scooter, "walking" his little dog on a leather leash in the middle of the road, the old man never even turned around. The big Buick bearing down on him didn't faze him because he was practically blind and had no idea she'd nearly squashed him like a palmetto bug with her enormous vehicle.

Gloria pounded the steering wheel while she waited on the old man. Better the steering wheel than the old man. She tooted her horn so he would know she was behind him and lingered only a few feet from the bumper of his golf cart. Wanting to get home to tell Jim about George but delayed by Mr. Tweeble's lack of concern for others on the road only added to the frustration building inside her. How had she not seen the old man with his round belly lapped over his belt and wearing a yellowed white shirt, black suspenders, and red plaid shorts? Knee high black dress socks and black dress shoes completed his usual attire. If she hadn't been thinking about George's death, she would've seen Mr. Tweeble sooner. How did she miss noticing him driving that red scooter and wearing that ugly outfit?

Gloria spotted her neighbor Ethel across the street, watching the whole scene with a slight smile on her face. Usually Ethel's gruff exterior never broke, but she seemed to be enjoying Gloria's frustrating situation.

After waiting for what felt like forever before she could get around the old man, Gloria passed Ethel and didn't even take time to wave. She continued down the street, then swung into her driveway and parked the Buick under the carport. She jumped out and opened the back door to grab her exercise equipment. Her hand slapped her forehead when she realized she'd left her mat at the community center. She stood staring at the lonesome bag on the seat. *Oh, Gloria, calm down.* She grabbed the bag, slammed the car door, and rushed from the carport through the back door to the kitchen.

Chapter Two

"Jim, Jim!" Gloria threw her keys and bag on the kitchen counter. She scurried through the kitchen to the tidy living room. "Jim!" She called louder. He wasn't in their small double-wide home.

Gloria retraced her steps through the kitchen and gingerly stepped down the steps from the kitchen to the carport. She darted into the attached shed housing the laundry room with storage in the front and Jim's workshop in back, then hurried through the workshop and out the door to the neat little back yard and found him watering their postage stamp-sized vegetable garden.

She marched up to her tall husband dressed in his old work clothes. "Did you hear about George MacDonnell?" Gloria shook her auburn hair, compliments of her favorite brand of hair color #118. Her clear blue eyes grew misty.

"Yes, I heard." Jim's dark brown eyes, filled with sadness, pierced her heart. He kinked the hose to stop the water flow and dragged it to the faucet on the back of the house. He turned the tap to cut off the stream of water and dropped the hose to the freshly cut grass.

"How sad he died alone. Do you know he wasn't discovered for so long his body just ro..." Her hands covered her face as she sobbed.

"Gloria, let's go in the house so we can talk about George." He touched the small of her back to direct her to the back door.

Gloria knew her husband of thirty-five years well enough to realize something wasn't right. He never stopped watering the garden until he was finished. And then, to ask her to come in the house instead of picking up his tools and carrying them into the shed was so unlike him.

As they stepped into the bright kitchen, Jim turned to her. Looking straight into her eyes, he said, "Royce called this morning. George's death was peculiar. Those are his exact words."

Jim was friends with the county M.E., Royce Williams. They met while working together on death calls in the community when the first responders were called to the scene. Living in a retirement community, the Medical Examiner and EMT's were frequent visitors. An ambulance at a home was not a significant event at Citrus Ridge. It was part of life, and death, in the senior park earning its name as "God's waiting room."

"Royce told us George's body didn't rot. It couldn't have decomposed that quickly because Miss Lottie checked on him every day when she brought him the mail in the afternoon. She delivered it the day before he died, and she told

Royce he was alert and talked about the weather.

"When Lottie found George, she left his house to avoid staring at the sight of his gruesome body and breathing in the putrid odor in the house. She went home and called 911 at one o'clock yesterday, but she was so emotional, she was unable to speak. They traced the call to her house. When the police arrived, she was so distressed she just pointed to George's house."

Jim stopped a minute to take a breath. Gloria touched his shoulder, wishing she knew what to do to soothe his anguish. "They discovered George sitting in the living room in his recliner. His body was mustard yellow. His clothes were melted to his body. The odor wasn't a rotting smell, more like burning or scorching. In fact the fabric in the chair was charred. Ron was the first responder." He hesitated before he went on. Clearing his throat, he said, "He told me when he and the paramedics touched the body, it turned to powder."

Gloria sucked in her breath. Her hands jerked to her chest. "Dear God. What happened, Jim? What could have caused that?"

Jim shook his head. "I don't know. No one knows. Ron arrived at the scene first. You know Ron. Always talking and telling great stories." Gloria remembered the usually fun-loving raucous Ron.

"Royce told me there was such a look of horror in Ron's eyes. He was traumatized by what he saw. Ron told him he moved George's wrist, and his hand fell making a pile of yellow ashes on the floor."

"Dear God." Her knees buckled, but Jim caught her and helped her walk into the dining room. He eased her down into the wooden chair at the table, concern etching his face. She swallowed hard to keep the nausea at bay.

Jim wiped his eyes with his fingers. "I don't know how Ron and Lottie will ever forget this nightmare."

The ominous feeling of inconceivable danger washed over her. Jim sat down heavily in the chair across from Gloria, reaching his hand across the table. She rested her hand lightly on his. After thirty-five years of marriage, she knew they needed no words; the touch was comfort enough to carry them through what she feared would be the difficult days ahead.

* * *

Unable to stop thinking about George, Gloria decided to take a walk in the afternoon sunshine, hoping the fresh air would lift the sorrow in her soul. As she passed Ethel's house, pangs of guilt for not waving back at Ethel earlier slammed her heart. Her frustration and bad mood caused by Mr. Tweeble rolling down the middle of the road was no excuse to be rude to Ethel.

Gloria walked up the concrete driveway to apologize to her and explain why she didn't take time to acknowledge her. As she entered the carport, she heard a scream inside Ethel's house. Gloria rushed to the back of the house and pounded on the door.

"Ethel, Ethel. Are you okay?" Gloria rattled the doorknob and found it was unlocked. She pushed the door open and entered Ethel's kitchen. "Ethel, it's Gloria. Are you okay? Where are you?" Gloria heard water running in the bathroom off the kitchen, so she made a beeline to the door.

"Ethel," she yelled, her voice filled with panic. Gloria's heart raced in her chest as she leaned over the unconscious woman in the bath tub. What should she do? She couldn't pull Ethel out of the bathtub by herself. Besides, she remembered there was something about not moving a fall victim. Her brow creased, knowing she couldn't leave her there. Her skeleton-like neighbor was lying splayed out in the tub full of water. At least she didn't land face down in the soapy water.

Gloria turned off the faucets and pulled the plug. The water swirled down the drain. She grabbed the bath towel lying on the toilet lid and wrapped it around Ethel. She pulled her up to a sitting position using the back of the tub as a prop. She held Ethel with one hand and grabbed her cell phone from her pocket with the other. Her trembling fingers managed to dial 911.

"911. What is your emergency?"

"Yes, hello. My neighbor has fallen and I can't get her up." Gloria removed her hand from Ethel's shoulder to push hard on her own temples, trying to alleviate the ache settling in her head. When Ethel started sliding sideways on the back of the tub, Gloria quickly grabbed her again and held her up.

The woman on the line asked, "What is your address?"

"Wait a minute. I can't hear you," Gloria shouted into her phone.

"Hush, Buttons!" She yelled at Ethel's yapping dog running in and out of the bathroom, adding more stress to the situation for Gloria. "Go on. Go on. Get out of here." She shooed the little mutt away from her, still clenching the phone in her hand.

"I'm sorry. There's a little dog here that's pretty excited. Buttons! Hush!" Gloria said.

"What is your address," the voice on the phone asked again.

Ethel moaned. She seemed to be coming to. "What the hell happened?" She blinked up at Gloria. "Dammit. Get me out of here."

Gloria gently held Ethel's shoulder, but when the determined woman struggled to get up, Gloria dropped the phone on the floor and firmly grasped Ethel's arms to hold her down. She didn't want her to stand up and then fall again, but this feisty eighty-something old lady was stronger than she looked.

"Stay there, Ethel. I've called for help. Just be patient." Fearing Ethel would hurt herself even more, Gloria struggled to hang onto her. She had no hands free to retrieve the phone from the bathroom floor and talk to the emergency operator, so she hollered Ethel's address at the phone and urged the 911 operator to get someone out there fast.

Trying to remain calm, she turned back to Ethel and asked, "Do you need another towel?"

Ethel's eyes narrowed as she gazed full on at Gloria. "Let me outta here, Gloria. Dammit! I'm okay. Why'd you call 911? Are those first responder clowns going to show up here?" Ethel's face twisted into an ugly frown. "Son of a bitch, I'm naked! I don't want them to see me like this. Dammit to hell. Let me outta this tub!"

"Calm down, Ethel." Still hanging on to Ethel's arms, she tried to change from her stooped position to her knees.

Relief swept over Gloria when she heard a woman's voice call from the kitchen door. "Where are you? I'm Leslie, a first responder. I'm here to help."

"In the bathroom. Hurry. Ethel's slipped and fallen in the tub."

Gloria was never so happy to see someone. Thank goodness it was her friend, Leslie.

"Dammit, girl. Let me get outta this tub!" Ethel continued to squirm but Gloria held her down, although her knees ached so badly she wouldn't be able to stay in the position for long.

"Oh, my side, my side hurts. Shit." Gloria felt Ethel stop resisting when the pain took over and she let her go. The injured woman closed her eyes and held her left side, but continued muttering every blue word Gloria had ever heard in her life. Evidently Ethel's ribs were more painful than the goose egg beginning to appear on the side of her head.

Gloria left Ethel in Leslie's care and emerged from the bathroom noticing more first responders, including her husband Jim, at the scene. With so many people in the small house, she was afraid Ethel's violet plants would be knocked over. She stood near Ethel's beloved plants to guard them as she answered all of the questions from the county EMT's when they arrived. It seemed to take forever to give the information.

She smiled when she heard Ethel yelling at the EMTs in her own very special way of addressing them as SOBs. But when they had her on the cot and wrapped up to keep her warm, she answered their questions about her summer home address in Ohio, her daughter's name, and her phone number in New York.

Gloria was happy to see her neighbor clear-headed and not in shock. She smiled as she watered the violets at the kitchen sink before she left. Ethel may be bruised and in pain, but she was a strong, stubborn woman who would overcome this slip and fall her own way.

When Gloria stepped outside into the Florida sunshine, she was surprised at the hubbub in front of Ethel's house. A fire engine, rescue squad vehicle, and an ambulance lined the curb. The first responders directed traffic at the intersections to bypass the block where Ethel lived on Lemon Avenue. A crowd of curious onlookers had gathered on the other side of the street, in fact in Gloria's front yard.

Gloria felt overwhelmed when the neighbors moved as a unit to surround her in the middle of the road and fired questions.

"What happened? Is she going to be okay? Is she conscious?" Gloria tried to answer each one.

"Who's got her dog?"

Oh, poor Buttons. Gloria had forgotten the yappy Yorkie. She glanced back toward the driveway and saw Jim carrying the frightened pet in his arms. Knowing her husband's love of dogs, she grinned at him as he hugged the little white dog to his chest.

"I promised Ethel I'd watch this little guy for her till she gets back from the hospital." Jim reminded Gloria of the days when her kids were young and found a stray. They would always plead, "Can we keep him?"

"I'm sure knowing you'll take care of Buttons is a big relief for her." Gloria, not exactly a dog lover, was not too thrilled about having a dog around to trip over and care for. Her winters were to be stress free, no schedules, and no responsibilities.

Of course, she missed the kids and grandkids. It would be fun to have the family visit so they could absorb the sunshine, hunt for shells and frolic on the beach while they escaped the cold, sunless Northern winter, but there were no plans for that to happen this year. In April she'd be ready to head back north yearning to see the grandchildren and join in the activities that were close to her heart. She certainly didn't want to ruin her carefree winter by being responsible for a neighbor's dog.

Chapter Three

Pamela squinted as she sized up the length of the path from the golf ball to the hole, happy to be on the golf course away from all the discussions about the horrible death of George McDonnell this morning. The afternoon sun gently warmed her. The lazy breeze wafted across the course just enough to give the palm trees a quiet sway. No clouds in the brilliant blue sky. The weather was perfect for golf, but Pamela's usually perfect game was far from perfect.

"I saw it break off to the right. It's got to be around here." Pamela shoved the shrub's branches out of the way with her golf club. Noel was on the other side of the bushes looking for her contrary ball. She had muffed the shot. Having everyone else in her group on the fairway or on the green see how badly she had hit the ball only added to her frustration with this game.

"Here it is, Pamela." Noel pointed to the ball sitting right under the bush between them. "That won't be such a bad shot. You can get on the green from here, kiddo." He winked and smiled at her.

She frowned and murmured to herself, "I doubt it."

Pamela and Wayne Gates of Ohio and Rosemary and Noel Woodcock from New York became winter friends when they purchased their homes at Citrus Ridge. Their similar interests in golfing, games, and socializing in the clubs in the community drew them together. If one couple attended an event, the other couple went with them. They had spent many winter days together on the golf course.

Pamela usually loved teeing off at the Citrus Ridge eighteen-hole golf course. The grounds were well kept, the fairways were short, and the numerous water hazards were not so large she couldn't hit over them. Of course, there were days like today when her game was off. She drove more than one ball into the rough and ricocheted one off a Florida Oak tree, narrowly missing another foursome. Another plopped into a water hazard she usually managed with her powerful drive.

"Okay, honey," her husband Wayne called to her. "Keep your head down. Don't try and kill the ball."

Steam seemed to escape through her ears. Not wanting to ruin their outing with their friends, she bit her tongue and clenched the club. She didn't need coaching from him on every shot.

Ignoring him, she shook her head to clear her thoughts and focus on the shot.

The other three stood behind her. "Did you hear all the people in George's house this morning have been quarantined?" Noel asked.

"Yeah, I guess they have no idea what killed George. Could be some disease," Wayne said with a shrug.

"At the crafts club luncheon, someone said the police think he could've been poisoned," Rosemary added.

Pamela whirled about with eyes staring daggers at them. "Will you guys be quiet? I'm trying to concentrate on my shot here!" They all stepped back a few paces.

"Sorry, honey, I didn't realize we were talking so loud we bothered you." All three exchanged amused glances after she turned her back to them.

"This must be a pretty big dangerous deal. Police are going to guard the house 24 hours a day to keep sightseers away," Wayne whispered.

Pam spun about again. "Wayne!"

"Jeez, you must have the ears of an owl, Pamela," he said.

Pamela, pumping her shoulders to loosen up her muscles and relieve her tension, turned away from her annoying playing partners. She adjusted her feet closer to the ball to take her shot.

She felt the sun blazing down on her squared shoulders and the eyes of the other players boring into her. Her game may be off, but at least she looked perfect in her white polo top decorated with appliquéd suns glowing as brightly as the yellow shorts that contrasted against her brown legs and arms.

With that thought, she swung. "Oh, nooooo." The ball sailed off into the sand trap.

"Aw, Pam—." He stopped mid-sentence when she turned and glared at her husband.

Don't say another word." Wayne and Rosemary remained quiet as she tromped toward the wayward golf ball.

After the seemingly endless game, Pamela plopped down on the chair under the umbrella table on the deck of the 19th Hole Bar, happy to be off that torturous golf course.

She and Rosemary waited for the guys to bring their drinks from the bar inside. She didn't feel like making small talk. She shook her head with the realization that even Rosemary had scored better than her for the day!

Rosemary usually was not a great golfer. Her round body and short legs and arms made it difficult for her to have a PGA swing. Pamela knew Rosemary would have been happier to work on her crafts, but she played the game to please Noel.

Pamela liked Noel. He was outgoing and friendly and always planning a gathering with friends. But Rosemary preferred a night at home in front of the TV. Pamela realized from Rosemary's conversations that the couple didn't share interests anymore nor did they share a bed together.

"I think the water hazards were your favorite spots today, Pam." Noel said as he took his seat across from her at the table.

"Not to mention the bushes." Placing the drinks on the table, Wayne grinned and slapped her on the shoulder.

Both men chortled as they saw Pam's face turn red with anger.

"Well, at least she looks good on the course," Noel said.

"Why, thank you, Noel, I think," she replied. She made a peevish face at him.

"Let's toast to another great game today…all except for Pamela's." Wayne raised his glass high. Everyone laughed except for her. Silence overcame the group until Noel offered to go after more drinks. Pamela's eyes flung icy daggers at her husband who quickly decided to join him.

* * *

A few nights later, Mr. Tweeble woke up with a start when his dog Jingles began barking loud enough to wake him even if he wasn't wearing his hearing aids.

"Jingles! Jingles! Hush up, will you? It's three o'clock in the morning. You're going to wake the neighborhood with your barking."

He remembered Jingles barking and whining like that when he drove his electric scooter near George McConnell's house that afternoon. He had finally picked up the feisty terrier and put him on his lap to join the other curiosity seekers near the house. The dog jumped off and raced the other way until he was brought up short on his leash and howled until his master turned the cart around and left the area.

Jingles' pitiful yowling broke into Mr. Tweeble's memory.

Fearing his dog was sick, Mr. Tweeble rolled himself out of bed, fumbled putting on his glasses, and shuffled into the kitchen. Using the night light in the hood vent over the old stove to see the dog, he discovered the animal scampering back and forth near the back door.

"Jingles, come 'ere, boy. Are you sick?" Mr. Tweeble picked him up and gently held the dog close to his chest. He switched on the ceiling light and studied the precious face he dearly loved. He checked Jingles' brown ears and his brown and white furry body for any injuries, and then cradled him to his rotund belly.

"It's all right, little guy. Come on. Come on to bed with me. You must want to go out to chase a rabbit, eh?" As he slowly shuffled his way back to his bedroom with the dog, he wondered what was wrong. Mr. Tweeble made a mental note to check behind the couch for an "accident" in the morning.

He lay down on the rumpled bed and enfolded the trembling dog in his arms. Suddenly Jingles wriggled free and sprang up barking non-stop. He leaped from the bed and raced out of the room. A flash of searing yellow light filled the room blinding Mr. Tweeble, and the smell of his own scorched flesh burned his nostrils.

Chapter Four

Mr. Tweeble's next door neighbor, Doris Hadley, couldn't sleep. She prowled through her cupboards to find a snack. Sometimes slurping up some raisin bran cereal and milk and watching a late night movie on the AMC channel made her sleepy. She filled her cereal bowl and settled into her recliner with the hope she would soon be dreaming sweet dreams.

Placing her spoon and bowl on the table next to the chair, she pulled her heavy robe around her thin body and sat down in her lounger. She clicked the remote and the TV across the room shined bright in the darkened room. Pleased to discover a favorite oldie on the classic movie channel, *Casablanca*, Doris traded the remote for her cereal and concentrated on watching the movie and indulging in the night time treat.

After a few minutes, she turned up the volume, and then again turned it louder. Ungluing her eyes from the TV screen, she realized the conversation between Humphrey Bogart and Ingrid Bergman was lost due to Mr. Tweeble's confounded dog barking and howling over the movie's audio.

Doris set aside her cereal bowl on the end table. She pulled her frail body from the deep seat ready to make a phone call to Ralph Tweeble to complain about the dog. Of course once she was up, the pet quit yapping. She looked out the window to scan Ralph's yard to see if he had let the dog out into the backyard, but the motion light wasn't on. She cocked her good ear toward his house and listened. Ah, silence from next door. Maybe now she could watch her movie without that annoying barking.

Doris picked up her cereal bowl and returned to the kitchen to fill it with more raisin bran and milk. She settled down in front of the maple TV console. As she brought a spoonful of her midnight snack to her lips, the terrier next door began raising the roof with his howls and yelps again.

She had enough of that damn dog. She wrestled herself up from the recliner as fast as her stiff body would allow and spied out the window. She stood mesmerized by a dazzling yellow light blazing through Old Man Tweeble's house. Momentarily blinded by the amazing brightness, she scrambled out to her screened-in porch to get a better view and caught a whiff of the most putrid odor she had ever smelled in her seventy-nine years on this earth.

Doris moved as quickly as her legs tolerated to call 911. Where was that dad-burned phone? Who ever thought of cordless phones anyway? When there were phones hooked up to the wall with a cord on the handset, no one ever missed a call because they couldn't find the damn thing. She was exasperated, but she was more scared the house next door might explode into flames if she didn't call right away.

Doris checked the kitchen table, the couch cushions and the night stand by the bed for the phone. Finally she found it where it should be…on the desk in the charger. She grabbed it and called 911.

"Come quick! There was a flash of bright light next door. Something's on fire!" Doris clutched her chest, unable to breathe. "Hurry!" Everything turned black as she passed out and fell to the floor, the phone clattering down next to her.

* * *

In that early morning, the first responders discovered two bodies in their respective homes on Sunshine Boulevard—Mr. Ralph Tweeble and Mrs. Doris Hadley. The aura of death and mystery overshadowed the dazzling sunny day.

Jim Hart and the burly Detective Samuel Parker huddled together in Mr. Tweeble's home discussing the unbelievable circumstances surrounding the man's death. After the Medical Examiner checked the body of Mrs. Hadley next door, he joined the discussion in Mr. Tweeble's unkempt living room, a museum of the history of the old man's life through pictures. The yellowing photos of his young family, a portrait of Tweeble in his Army uniform, and a certificate honoring him for his work in the Rotary Club hung on the walls. On the cluttered table next to his recliner, a small bag of marijuana sat next to a framed photo of Tweeble and his wife in front of a fiftieth anniversary cake.

The tall, slender Medical Examiner, Royce Williams, easy to spot in the crowd, motioned to an EMT and instructed him to go ahead and bag the body since it had cooled enough to handle. They tried to keep as much of it intact as possible. Tweeble's body had begun to flake away in a few areas. It had not disintegrated into yellow powder as McDonnell's body had, but it was mustard yellow and emitted a sickening odor.

"I've been doing this job for the past twelve years and have never seen yellow bodies like this. We need to get out of the house. There may be toxic air in here." The masks over their faces did nothing to filter the foul odor. They made their way outdoors where the stink lay heavy in the air.

Police had cordoned off a large area around the house so the gathering crowd could not get near the crime scene. Moving away from the house, Jim, Detective Parker, and the M.E. Royce Williams moved to a yard across the street and gazed at the double-wide home. No sign of fire or damage was evident.

The three men stood in a circle facing each other. The trained detective and medical examiner's faces were drawn and pale as they talked together. The shock of seeing a human being in that condition had even sickened the professionals who saw death every day. Did they want to run away when they saw the garish scene of death like he wanted to? The horrible sight was forever branded into his memory. His stomach still churned when he recalled the image in the Tweeble's bedroom.

Jim's lips compressed across his teeth. "My God, Royce. What happened in there?" Royce held his palms out in front of him and shook his head.

"I have no explanation yet. I did a quick assessment of the old man's body and found holes on his wrists," Royce pointed to the inside of his left wrist, "but no other lacerations or wounds. Of course, once we get him on the table, the forensic guys will examine him thoroughly." He straightened his back and took a deep breath. "The desiccation throws me. There's no evidence of accelerant, matches, cigarettes. The charred area is only around the body. The rest of the mattress was warm but not burned. It's like a hot flash went through his body.

"We'll need more lab work and forensics than our county has in its facilities." Royce faced Parker. "We need to call the State Police now, Sam, and report these unusual deaths to the NIH. I don't know if we're dealing with a disease, environmental pollution, an insect problem, or who knows what else. I have no clue to the cause of such a ghastly death. The departments may have had similar cases and could have answers for us."

"Okay. We've worked with them several times with no problems in the past. I'm sure they'll be willing to help us with the investigation," said Parker. His light brown face showed no emotion, but his dark brown eyes reflected his distress.

Royce drew the palm of his hand down from his forehead to his chin before speaking again. "The holes in the wrists will be tested to ascertain if that has anything to do with the death, as well as any fluids. Basically, the body has no fluids left. I think they boiled away in the heat."

Royce shook his head. He gulped another breath of air.

"The police are notifying next of kin for Ms. Hadley and Ralph," Jim said. "I know you don't want anything disturbed. So when can I tell the relatives they can get into the houses?"

"I don't know!" Royce snapped. His fierce retort surprised Parker and Jim.

Dropping his long arms to his sides, Royce said, "Sorry, guys. I'm at my wit's end. I really don't know how to figure it all out. I'm looking forward to help from the forensic lab."

Jim clapped Royce on the back. He also felt the frustration and anger he knew was bothering Royce. To see a human being die like that was more than disturbing. Was Mr. Tweeble tortured with pain before he died or was he dead the minute from whatever caused his death? Jim tried to swallow the knot forming in his throat. He couldn't ask Royce these questions because he'd had enough. Hadn't they all had enough?

Tweeble's barking dog interrupted the men's conversation. "Here, Jingles. Jingles, come 'ere." Jim squatted down and motioned to the Jack Russell terrier. Jingles only woofed and backed away. He tore around the bushes and then ran away from the men, crossing the street and then disappearing as he raced behind Tweeble's house.

"That's Ralph's dog. He must be scared to death. Let's catch him." The three men headed to the back yard. As they approached, Jingles turned his nose up, sniffing the air. When he saw them coming, he playfully dodged them. Each one lunged for the pet but came up short. Parker hurled himself after the dog and fell flat on the St. Augustine grass. Royce's suit coat flapped in the wind as he chased the nimble pet.

Jingles stopped dead in his tracks. He picked up something from under the sturdy bush and tossed it up in the air.

"Oh, you want to play, do ya?" Jingles stood still. "What have you got there?" Jim asked.

Growling, the little dog picked up the object, shook it violently, and flung it away. He ran after it and returned to Jim, clenching it between his teeth. Jingles lay down and deposited a lifeless snake at Jim's feet as if he were offering him a gift.

"Ah, good dog. Good dog. You caught a snake." Jim grabbed the dog's collar and held him tight.

"Shoot. We need those black snakes here. They're great for my garden," he said.

"That isn't a black snake. I've never seen one with three yellow stripes down its back like that. Have you?" Royce kicked the snake away from him.

"My God, do you know how many snakes there are in Florida? There's one of every size, color, and length here, and variations of each species. My wife hates 'em, and I figure the only good snake is a dead snake." Parker nodded and pinched his lips together.

"I think I saw a leash tied to the front porch." Jim picked up Jingles and hugged him. "I'll get the leash, but the next question is who gets to take this little doggie home?"

Royce and Parker looked at each other. They both turned toward Jim and said, "You!"

* * *

In the late afternoon, trying to distract her mind from the horrific deaths discovered that morning, Gloria walked around the neighborhood to burn off the anxiety building in her about the mysterious deaths. She hoped the cause wasn't contagious. When flu hit the community, it affected many residents. Some weren't strong enough to survive the merciless epidemic.

38

Gloria closed her eyes and breathed to help her erase the negative thoughts. Determined to enjoy the outdoors, she dwelled on the beautiful day and patted herself on the back knowing she was walking to keep the pounds off her thighs, strengthen her heart, and lower her cholesterol. She would do anything in order to not take prescription medicine. Not only for the expense, but also questionable about how the drugs might affect her body.

As she fast-walked past Ethel's house, Ethel stood watching out her kitchen window that faced the road. Ethel always paid attention to what happened in the neighborhood with views through her large windows, her form of entertainment. Gloria didn't mind her snooping and in fact, she smiled, realizing Ethel must be doing fine after her fall.

Gloria stopped to greet the neighbor who lived a couple of houses away from hers on the same side of the street as their house. She stepped from the road onto his thick green lawn near the curb. "Hi, Paul. How are you?"

Paul looked up from watering the azalea bushes and flowering plants in front of his house. She crossed the lawn to talk to him.

"I can't complain much. Beautiful weather this morning. I don't mind it on the cool side. How are you?"

"Oh, I'm fine," she answered as usual. No one really asks how a person is to hear a list of problems. And she certainly didn't want to bring up unpleasant conversation about the mysterious deaths on Sunshine Boulevard.

"I enjoy walking by your yard. Everything is so pretty and green here." She waved her hands toward the landscape of lush native shrubs lining the sides and front of his home. Even his back yard was full of healthy green plants and perennials. He had a green thumb for sure. She and Paul enjoyed sharing cuttings and exchanging advice on growing plants in the Florida climate. They were different than the plants she grew in northern summers.

Paul pulled on the hose to move farther along the bed of azaleas. "Well, your yard is looking healthy this winter too. It's been a good year for growing—well until we had to cover up a few nights to save the plants from the cold snap."

It had been a cold couple of weeks with an unusual amount of freezing nights this season. They both were tired of blanketing the plants susceptible to the unusual frosty Florida nights.

"Are you going to cover your plants tonight?" Gloria laughed.

Paul grinned. "Finally, we don't have to drag out the sheets to protect them from the cold, huh?"

She nodded. Although it was a lot of work to cover the plants, but it was worth it. So far they were staying healthy.

He smiled an engaging smile. "How's Buttons?"

"Oh, that's pretty sad when you ask about the dog and not about Ethel." Gloria grinned. "She got home from the hospital yesterday afternoon. Pretty sore, but she insisted on taking Buttons back home so she could care for him. Jim plans to walk the dog for a few days, but actually, it's a good excuse so he can keep an eye on Ethel too. The docs are watching her for signs of a concussion."

"She's a very lucky lady not to have a broken bone or two in that fall," he said. "But she's a tough old bird." He winked. Gloria grinned believing he had said what everyone thought about Ethel. But then, Paul was an honest guy and never held back his opinions on topics.

Gloria liked Paul and his wife, Barb. She and Jim were about the same age as the fun couple, but that was the only way they were alike. Both couples attended dances at the community center and golf parties at the club, but Paul and Barb always stayed till they turned off the lights. She admired them for their easy going lifestyle. Paul, a Vietnam War vet, never let go of the 70's, keeping his long pony tail, now coarse and gray.

Gloria secretly wished she and Jim could jump on a Harley motorcycle to join them on one of their bike excursions to explore Florida. She loved hearing about their adventures.

She waved at Barb as she headed to the laundry room in the shed attached to the double-wide trailer home. Barb juggled the laundry basket and waved back, then disappeared through the doorway.

Paul kinked the hose to stop the water flow and stepped closer to Gloria. "I have a favor to ask of you and Jim." He shrugged. "You can say no if you want to. No problem."

Gloria's curiosity peaked when she saw him dart his eyes to the shed to check for his wife.

"I'm going to surprise Barb with an early anniversary gift, a cruise to the Bahamas. Would you and Jim have time to water our plants while we're gone for seven days?"

"Hmmm…let me think a minute…" Gloria's eyes danced as she waited a beat.

"Well, I can call you before we leave to check with you. But if you can't….."

"Oh, Paul. What are neighbors for? Of course, we'll take care of them. I understand your concern. It's very dry this year and no rain forecasted for this week, not to mention these cold nights."

"That's great! Thanks, Gloria. You've made my day. I'll call you the day before we leave to check in with you."

"That'd be a good idea, but with all the craziness around here, we aren't planning to leave anytime. So we'll be here. Any special instructions I should know about?"

"Not really. Just water if you need to. And you know where the hoses are for that."

"Hopefully we've seen the last of the cold weather. But just in case, do you keep the blankets in the back shed?"

"Oh, yeah. You can't miss the huge pile of them in the back of the shed." He grinned. Now don't tell Barb about the cruise, okay?" He put his finger to his lips.

"Cross my heart. Your surprise is safe with me. I hope you have a great time on the cruise."

* * *

While preparing dinner that evening, Gloria switched on the small TV on a stand in the dining room just off the kitchen. Every week night they watched the evening news like a nightly ritual. Jim brought in the hamburgers from the grill outside, and then they both sat down at the table.

Jim had no appetite after experiencing the horrific scene at Tweeble's home. The smell of the home embedded in his nose made him feel sick even now. He only wanted a glass of water and to listen to the news.

The perfectly dressed anchorman with a sprayed and waved haircut, handsome tan face, and neon white teeth faced the camera with a practiced look of concern.

"Tonight. Breaking news. We turn to the scene of two deaths in the retirement community of Citrus Ridge. Reporter Heather Blake is on the scene. What can you tell us tonight concerning these latest deaths, Heather?"

Heather stood in front of one of the double-wide homes in Citrus Ridge framed by tall palms. Her tight turquoise sweater hugged her shapely body; the color complimented her sparkling blue eyes.

"Thanks, Skyler. Mr. Ralph Tweeble, age seventy-eight, and his neighbor, Mrs. Doris Hadley, age seventy-nine, were found dead this morning in their homes on Sunshine Boulevard in this usually peaceful Citrus Ridge Senior Community. According to reliable sources, Mrs. Hadley called 911 to report a fire next door. Responders found Mrs. Hadley dead on the floor in her office. Mr. Tweeble was found at his home in his bedroom." Heather read from the notes on her tablet, and then faced the camera blinking her long eye lashes, set off with her perfectly shadowed and outlined eyes.

"The police have the area sectioned off and haven't given us any information on the cause or time of the deaths. You may recall this community lost a resident recently, Mr. George McConnell. No one is saying the three deaths are related.

"We'll update you at eleven. From Sunshine Boulevard in Citrus Ridge Senior Community, this is Heather Blake, News Channel Eight. Back to you, Skyler." With a huge smile, she rushed through the sign-off before she could be cut off.

Jim clicked off the TV channel with the remote as he stood up from the dining room table. "Seeing the reporter standing there reporting almost gleefully about people dying here turns my stomach," he said.

"Me too. But there's nothing we can do about it." Gloria balled up her paper napkin and pitched it on her plate.

With sarcasm oozing through his voice, he said, "And isn't that just great she gave the location? Now every curiosity seeker will be down here to snoop, and all the wannabe detectives will try to get in here to solve the case."

Jim grabbed the plates and piled them together with a loud clattering and heaped on the dirty silverware and salt and pepper shakers. He tried to balance the glasses on top of all that as he turned away from the table. Gloria rescued them before they fell and crashed on the tile floor.

"For Pete's sake, Jim, calm down," she said. He ignored her and marched toward the kitchen, but stopped and peered through the front windows to watch the traffic outside on their street. "There go more sightseers and another TV truck and more police cars down the street."

Shaking his head in disbelief, he turned his back on the scene outside and carried the dishes to the small kitchen piling them next to the pans Gloria had placed near the sink. "I think the crowds are getting bigger. People act like this is a carnival show."

He faced Gloria. "I'm glad the cops are here in the park. Our volunteer security can't begin to handle all the loonies swarming through the neighborhoods."

The traffic in and around the community from curious onlookers clogged streets creating traffic jams usually reserved for the big cities. Getting from Sunshine Boulevard to their home on Lemon Avenue took forever. Mobile TV station trucks claimed areas in the community center parking lots, and their helicopters droned above the neighborhood.

Jim grabbed a clean dish towel out of the drawer, but his thoughts had nothing to do with drying dishes. He was lost in the memory of seeing Tweeble's dog Jingles caged and placed in the animal control truck. The dog's frightened yelps and sad whining still echoed in his ears. Jim nearly shoved the officer aside to rescue Jingles, not wanting Jingles to be subjected to the isolation of the quarantine.

He shuddered to think of the possible deadly infections or diseases the dog may have picked up from being in the house with Tweeble at the time of his death. No one was sure if animals could be infected by whatever was killing the humans. Jim worried about the lovable dog with an uncertain future.

After George McDonnell's death earlier, everyone at the disaster scene was quarantined for seventy-two hours. Since Jim handled

Jingles, he was again on notice not to leave his house for twenty-four hours. At least he didn't have to stay in the hospital after the doctor's examination this time.

Jim and Gloria worked silently washing and drying the dishes and putting them away. "You're pretty quiet tonight," she said to him.

"Yeah." The gruesome scene he witnessed at Mr. Tweeble's home played in his head. The deaths haunted him. He wanted to tell Gloria. He wanted to find comfort and peace and eliminate the sadness by feeling her arms around him. But he knew if he started opening his heart to her, he wouldn't be able to stop the tears long enough to give voice to his fears. He wanted to tell her he was considering resigning from his volunteer duties as a first responder, but he couldn't even talk about it, not even to Gloria.

Chapter Five

As Gloria drove to Rosemary and Noel's home the next afternoon, the shimmering sun blazed down on the Citrus Ridge Senior Community.

Palm trees, oak trees and tropical shrubs dominated the landscaping of the double-wide trailer homes. Various statues of dolphins, manatees, and pelicans adorned the individual yards. Metal sun sculptures hung on walls of many of the homes. Each property included a carport attached to the home and a screened-in porch required by the by-laws of the community. Many of the screened in porches were converted to sunrooms with plastic or glass windows and enclosed walls and nicknamed Florida rooms.

The comfortable homes housed active baby boomers, retirees from all walks of life: dentists, medical doctors, ministers, business executives, farmers, truck drivers, couples married for fifty plus years, newlywed seniors, and unmarried couples who would lose pensions if they married.

Residents also included swinging single men who kept Viagra in their pockets in case they got lucky. Lots of single women due to the death of their spouse or divorce made advances to the available men and to the married men, drinking and dancing with them at the community center and karaoke bars. But the unsolved murders colored the carefree feeling in the once lively community and the pallor of death overshadowed the usual winter activities of the residents.

* * *

Deciding to forget the deaths and sadness of the last few days, Gloria drove her Buick along Sunshine Boulevard, the main street that circled the perimeter of the community. All of the circular roads in the park eventually led to or crossed Sunshine Boulevard. The woods on the north side, the guard shack on the east side, the protected conservation area on the south, and the small shopping mall on the west were landmarks to help her get her bearings in the development of over twelve hundred homes.

The striking tropical plants, the colorful flowers along her route and the bright sky above lifted her spirits. She chuckled under her breath remembering how her school teacher sister had called to report a snow day for her school due to a huge snowstorm. Feeling a bit guilty about reveling in the freedom she felt without the worry of sliding through ice and snow, she appreciated her snowbird status allowing her the luxury of winters in Florida.

Although she and Jim had owned the hardware business in their small town for twenty-five years, selling it was the best choice they had ever made. They put in enough hours there to have totaled fifty years of labor for the ordinary worker. Being a small business owner and your own boss was not all it was cracked up to be. It required hard work and lots of time, but they reaped the benefits of living comfortably and raising their family in a caring community.

Gloria pulled into Rosemary and Noel's driveway. She noticed Rosemary's car was gone. *Well, I'll just leave Rosemary's dishes on the steps if they're not home.* She picked up the empty casserole dish and glass cake pan from the passenger seat and walked up to door, the entrance to the kitchen.

Juggling the pans in one hand, Gloria rang the doorbell and knocked. She never trusted doorbells to work. She peeked through the small window in the door, then checked the door to see if it was locked. It was. Gloria bent down to leave the items on the top step when Noel arrived at the door.

"Oh, hi, Gloria." He opened the door and stood looking at her as she stood up. He was barefoot, shirtless, no belt in his shorts, and no smile.

"I hope I didn't disturb you."

"Well, I was going to take a nap. You caught me before I was snoring."

She was dazzled by the smile that eventually radiated across his handsome face. The mane of silver gray hair accented his tanned features. She felt a bit uncomfortable interrupting him.

"I wanted to return these dishes to Rosemary. She brought them over for the potluck. Is she here?"

"No, she's shopping. You know she can't miss a big sale at Beall's. Here. I can take those." He leaned down to get the dishes.

He stepped back and nearly tripped on a pair of gold sandals near the doorway. "Oh, no, now watch me break these. Rosemary will not be happy." He grinned again. "Thanks, I'll tell her you dropped them off. Good-bye." He grasped the door knob and began pushing the door closed.

Gloria laughed, feeling nervous just standing on the door step. "Well, you take care now and have a nice nap. We'll see you at the dance tonight, I guess?"

"Oh, sure. Glad you guys are coming. See ya' later." Gloria moved back as he shut the door. She shrugged. He was in a hurry to take his nap.

She backed her car carefully out of the driveway. Something nagged at her. What was wrong? A dark cloud covered the sun as she drove home.

* * *

That evening, seniors packed the Community Center. The abundance of gray and white hair and stiff bodies were the only clues this was not a high school homecoming dance. The music thundered, although there was no hip hop or rap music blaring over the speaker system. Instead, a three-piece band played the crowd favorites from the 50's and 60's. The energy was high, the conversations were loud, and the dancing was a mixture of practiced grace and raucous lunacy to the Golden Oldies tunes of love songs, rock and roll, and country twangers.

As soon as the first few bars played, people flooded the dance floor. Line dancing to *Boot Scootin' Boogie* and gyrating to the *Twist* with all the right classic moves, the men provided a lively show dressed in jeans, suits, and cowboy shirts while the women wore shorts, capris, dresses and skirts. Each table boasted a feast of snacks and finger foods prepared by the attendees. If you didn't want to dance, you could always eat. Various beverages sat on the table from assorted flavors of pop to fine wines and whiskey.

Gloria and Jim arrived early to take their places at their reserved table of eight. Gloria gave herself points for being early for once. Simon Veenstra joined them.. He leaned his canes on the table near his chair and maneuvered his stiff body into the seat. He had suffered a stroke that left his right leg paralyzed, but that didn't stop him and his wife, Evelyn, from attending each party and holding each other close as they danced in place.

"Hi, Simon. Where's Evelyn?"

"She'll be along. She's parking the car." A few minutes later, Evelyn joined them at the table with a bag full of goodies for the evening.

"Hi, Gloria. Hey, Jim." Evelyn Veenstra greeted them as she placed her bowl of dip and bag of chips on the table with the wine bottle and glasses. She came around the table to give Gloria and Jim big hugs.

"We saw Simon and were just watching for you."

Evelyn focused on Gloria's eyes. "I let Simon out at the door then park the car way out in the boondocks. You know, I never really appreciated it when Simon used to drop me off at the door and park the car." A wave of sadness passed between them. The stroke had altered not only his life, but also Evelyn's, not only in big ways, but in all ways in their lives together. Evelyn recovered quickly and remarked, "Looks like we already have a great crowd here."

"There, over there...Pam and Wayne." Gloria motioned to them to come over to her table. "And there are Rosemary and Noel right behind them."

Pamela, as usual, looked stunning in her black jumpsuit tightly cinched at her waist accentuating her trim figure. Her gold hoop earrings perfectly matched with her gold evening bag and sandals.

Gold sandals. Gloria's mind raced. She had seen those exact gold sandals someplace. Her stomach twisted into a knot. Noel tripped over those sandals when she returned Rosemary's casserole dish and cake pan.

Chapter Six

A few nights later, TV reporter Heather Blake waited for her cue from the TV studio to give her nightly report from Citrus Ridge. The softly lighted community center offered a peaceful backdrop for the news this evening of more deaths in the ravaged community. Jim watched her as she smoothed her long blonde hair and wet her red lips before facing the TV camera. He paced back and forth nervous about his upcoming interview with her.

In the studio, the anchorman said, "In the past weeks, the Citrus Ridge Retirement Community lost three of its residents. The investigation is ongoing. Tonight we turn to the scene of yet two more deaths in this senior community. Heather Blake is there with breaking news. What's happening out there tonight, Heather?"

The camera focused in on her sober face. "Thank you, Skyler. Two more bodies were discovered this morning at Citrus Ridge bringing the count up to five losses in this close-knit community. The police are not releasing information about the circumstances. From sources that we cannot reveal, it seems the police have not determined the causes of the previous deaths in this residential community.

"I have with me Jim Hart, Captain of the Citrus Ridge Community First Responders team." The camera captured Jim's image on the screen. He faced the reporter instead of looking into the camera lens, as instructed by the producer.

"Thank you for taking your time to be here, Mr. Hart. First responders are the ones first on the scene when you receive an emergency call here at Citrus Ridge. Is that correct?"

"Yes, the First Responders are volunteers with basic first aid training. We live in the park so we're able to make it to a home here in as little as two or three minutes. Often our quick response to an emergency means the difference between life and death for a person in need of care."

"Have you been called to the homes of those who have died due to an unknown cause?"

"Yes, we have." Jim looked down at his feet for a moment and then back to face Heather Blake.

"What can you tell us about these scenes when you arrive?" Her dark blue eyes captivated him. "Jim, can you describe the scenes when you arrive?"

"Well." He cleared his throat and tried to focus on the question. "I'm not at liberty to discuss the details of the ongoing investigations, however, I can tell you the local agencies are working together closely with the FBI and the

State Police. These officers and officials are determined to find out about these incidents."

"Thank you, Mr. Hart, and thank you for the lifesaving work you and your volunteers do for the residents in this area." Jim nodded at Heather to acknowledge her appreciation of their work. He didn't know if he was unable to talk because of his anguish about the deaths or because Heather's beautiful smile and tight sweater made him feel as nervous as a thirteen-year-old boy inviting a girl to the homecoming dance.

The TV screen filled with a close-up shot when she turned to the camera. "Our sources tell us no suspicious bacteria or diseases have been discovered. The authorities are checking the environment for air quality and water contamination. The police need you, the public, to call them if you have any information concerning any of these cases. Heather Blake reporting from Citrus Ridge. Back to you, Skyler."

The bright lights turned off, and Jim continued to stand near Heather. Although she was near his daughter's age, her beauty enchanted him.

"Thank you, Mr. Hart." She offered her hand for a handshake.

He grabbed her hand. "Oh, thank you, Heather, if I may call you Heather."

She smiled and nodded as she released her grip on his hand. "Oh, yes, Jim. I'm sure we'll be seeing more of each other. I mean as far as these unsolved cases go." A surge of electricity shot through his body when she smiled at him. "May I call and check with you as a resource for stories I'm working on?"

"Oh, of course. If I can tell you anything, I'd be glad to help." He wiped his sweaty palms on his pants legs. "We'd make a good team."

"Will it be okay if I drop by your house and talk with you and your wife sometime?"

Jim's eyes widened. Her question brought him back to the reality that he had a wife at home. "Oh, yeah, anytime. G'nite."

* * *

"Oh, my word, Jim. At exercise class this morning, everyone said don't drink the water because it's contaminated, and we should wear masks to protect us from the pollutants in the air." Gloria shoved her mat and bag loaded with the two pound barbells into the closet. Jim watched her as she walked to the sink and filled a glass with water from the tap and then dumped it down the drain.

"How do all these crazy stories get started?" She turned, empty glass in hand, and waited for his answer.

"I think everyone is discussing the deaths at every party, meeting, and neighborhood gossip group. Some of the stories are made up out of thin air. Look at the report that Mrs. Hadley shot herself when she found Mr. Tweeble dead." Jim pulled the coffee pot from the coffee maker and drained it to make it the fourth cup that morning.

"I think the air quality story started because the houses smell so bad from the dead bodies," she said.

Jim winced as he remembered his experiences from being at the death scenes. "The odor does make your stomach turn over," he said. He stared into his coffee mug. It was impossible for him to block the memories from his brain. He looked up and caught Gloria's sorrowful look on her face. "Let's not talk about it anymore, please."

She looked at the empty glass in her hand. "Huh. I don't remember drinking that glass of water."

"Hon, you didn't. You must be upset." He took the few steps to her and patted her shoulder. "Believe me, this will be over soon. I have no doubt the investigation will discover who or what is killing the people here."

Gloria reached for Jim and embraced him. He wrapped her in his arms and they stood quietly in the healing silence of their kitchen. They had stood together during difficult times in their many years of marriage and made it through. But this time, he didn't want to tell Gloria how the authorities really had no leads and no assurance there would ever be any answers to the cause of the deaths.

Jim was a volunteer fire fighter in his hometown in Michigan for twenty-five years and helped the local undertaker remove bodies.

Not in all his experience or in his forty-hour training class as a First Responder did anyone tell him what to do when a body was mustard yellow and deteriorated into a pile of yellow ashes. Jim recognized the smell of death, but the bodies smelled so putrid Jim knew the deaths were not natural.

"The Entertainer" ringtone sounded on his cell phone, a call from the Medical Examiner. "Hi, Royce. Sure, what time? Okay, I'll see you then."

Pushing the cell phone in his pocket, he said, "Royce wants me to meet him at Tweeble's house in fifteen minutes. Guess I have to put off that trip to the Wal-Mart with you, hon." He grinned at her. It was one of his least favorite places to go.

"Oh, dear." Gloria raised her hands to her cheeks flashing a sorrowful face. "I'll just have to go and spend all that money all by myself." A cheesy smile spread across her lips.

* * *

When Jim arrived at Tweeble's place, he found Royce and Parker strolling around the front lawn. The police tape still encircled the property and closed off the doors and windows. There were no flowers or lawn ornaments. A few unkempt bushes and a citrus tree struggled to survive in the old man's yard.

"I imagine people have been snooping around here even with the police tape up,"

Royce said. He removed his sunglasses to look closely along the side of the house.

Jim followed the men to the back yard where they stopped to talk to him.

"Why did you ask me to meet you here?"

"Do you remember when we investigated the house on the afternoon of Tweeble's death and found his dog in the back yard?" Parker asked.

"Yeah. He's a lively little dog. I remember chasing him down."

"Do you remember the dog killing the snake?"

"A black snake, wasn't it?"

Parker ignored Jim's question. "We're looking for that snake. We were about here when we saw the dog. I think he finally dropped it in front of us there." Parker pointed to the area near the bush.

"I hope it's still here," Royce said.

The three men searched the bushes, the weeds, and under the holly bush in the yard. "Why do you want the snake? Is the dog sick?"

"No, the dog's fine. The county released it to a family last week."

"That *is* good news, and he has a new family, too. That's great."

Parker continued. "Royce checked the victim's autopsy reports. He discovered the bodies have small holes through the skin. From what we can deduce, they're similar to snake bites. The problem is that when some snakes bite, a person won't even notice it. They aren't painful, unless the snake really wants to hurt you. If you don't feel it, the snake can keep biting you."

"But snakes only attack when they're cornered. They'd rather run away than strike." Jim stared at his two friends in disbelief. "You can't mean you are investigating that a snake killed these people."

Royce and Parker stopped looking in the dried grass for a minute. "Yes, it's a possibility the snake killed these people." Jim's surprise registered across his face.

Parker shook his head. "I know it sounds absolutely ridiculous, but that's the theory we're looking at now. There's similar evidence from the last three bodies. The first body was too decomposed to tell us much, though."

"So did this little snake try to eat a whole person? Come on, guys."

"We don't know why the snake's behavior is changing and becoming so aggressive. They're attacking people with no provocation."

"We have noticed that with each successive death, the snake bites on the bodies are larger. The snakes are getting bigger," Royce said.

"Oh, my God. Wait'll the media gets hold of this story. They'll spin this into a real sci-fi thriller." Jim laughed until he looked at his friends' solemn faces. He crossed his arms across his chest. "You guys are serious, aren't you? You believe this is a valid cause of death? That a snake would somehow get into a person's home and bite him without him knowing it or feeling symptoms of the venom?"

"Yes, and we have to find this nest of snakes before they procreate a whole new species of man killers," Royce said. Jim whistled like he did when he was a kid.

"It's extremely important this is not made public until we can corroborate the cause of death. Please keep it under your hat, Jim. We trust you with this information." Parker's eyes conveyed his sincerity.

"You can count on me," he said. "Thank you for explaining what we're doing here. I get it."

The men combed the yard and walked around the neighboring yards before gathering again in Tweeble's back yard. Jim felt the eyes of the curious neighbors peeking through their windows at them.

Parker quietly said out of the corner of his mouth, "Don't look over there, but I spotted the dead snake at the back of the property."

Jim tried hard not to look. When Gloria told him not to look at something, it was a sure thing he'd have to. He wiped his forehead with the back of his hand and glanced in that direction. "Sorry, guys." He smiled sheepishly.

Parker ignored his apology and strolled over to the bush. He removed a pair of latex gloves from his pocket and snapped them on his hands. As he casually surveyed the area, he produced a small bag from his back pocket. Quick as a flash he bent down and reached under a large bush. Using his body and the bush as a shield for privacy, he collected the decomposing snake and deposited the remains into the black plastic bag. He walked over to Royce and said loudly, "Well, we can't find anything here. Let's go."

Parker's weak attempt at acting didn't convince Jim. He knew him well enough to know he had found something important. Good thing Parker decided to be a detective and not an actor.

"No, I guess there's nothing here. Might as well get back to the office." Royce joined the charade as Jim tried to act cool for the benefit of the nib-nose neighbors.

Parker opened the trunk of his car and deposited the bag and his plastic gloves into a five-gallon bucket with a tight fitting lid. Before getting in the car, Royce shook Jim's hand. "Thanks, Jim. It's important to solve this and to do it quickly. I'll keep you posted, and you keep us informed on anything you see here."

"Sure will." Jim pumped Royce's hand wondering what might happen next on Sunshine Boulevard.

* * *

That night, Gloria clicked off the TV and reported the night's freezing temperatures forecast to Jim. They would have to cover their vegetable plants in the garden and flowers in the planters in front.

She found Jim changing the windshield wiper blade on the car in the carport. "Bad news, hon. Freezing temps tonight."

Jim frowned at her and she laughed. "Welcome to warm, sunny Florida, eh?"

"Well, let's get the sheets and blankets out. Then we'll have to cover Paul's plants and move the pots of plants from the back of the house into his shed. I don't know how tender they are, but I know he moves them in during a cold spell. Then we'd better cover the potted annuals. The front and side bushes are under cover and close enough to the house. They'll be okay," he said.

"Now I wish I'd asked him more about what he does, but I guess he figures we know what to do with everything since we have plenty of plants here to worry about."

Gloria turned toward the shed as she struck off to gather the materials to wrap up the garden for the night. "Where'd you put the key to Paul's shed? I'll get it when we're done covering here."

Gently returning the windshield wiper to its position, he said, "I didn't get his key. I thought you did."

Gloria stopped and whirled around to face her husband. "You're kidding, aren't you?"

"No. You made all the arrangements with Paul. You guys didn't think about a key to the shed in case we need to get in?" Gloria shook her head in disbelief. After thirty-five years of marriage, they still had issues with communication.

* * *

Jim tested the knob on the back door of Paul's shed. "All locked up."

"Yeah, all the doors are locked. Now what are we going to do? The big plants in the back are going to freeze right off. I certainly don't have enough sheets and blankets to cover those big pots." Gloria fanned her bangs back across her forehead. Guilt for not making better plans with Paul washed over her.

"Jeez, Gloria." He shook his head. "Well, the only thing to do is take them back to our house. I'll get the truck to transport them down there, and we'll put them in our shed for the night. We might as well keep 'em till Paul gets back. There may be more frosty nights ahead."

"Well, all I can say is, it better freeze tonight or all this will be for nothing!" Gloria's forehead creased with frustration.

"I'll get the truck and grab a few more old towels to cover up the geranium pots. Then we can load these in the back of the truck."

Gloria and Jim crammed the eight pots of healthy green plants into their small shed and shut the door to keep out the cool wind. "I can feel the temps falling since we started this. I'm going to make some coffee to warm us up."

Jim started to speak, but Gloria already knew what he wanted. "Yes, decaffeinated, since it's so close to bed time." He nodded his head. Scary that they had lived together so long she could read his thoughts. Or was that a good thing?

Chapter Seven

Jim and Gloria met up with their friends Wayne and Pamela at the golf course on Saturday evening. The Florida Chamber of Commerce bragged about nights like these with the warm breeze, and no humidity, not nearly as chilly as a few nights ago.

Jim tilted his head toward the clear sky filled with glittering stars and a bright full moon. "Just the right amount of light to illuminate the golf course for the midnight golf tournament," he said.

"Yeah," said Wayne, "but I'll probably still lose my ball out there."

"Look how pretty the golf course looks in the moonlight," Gloria said.

"Kind of magical and mysterious looking, isn't it," Pamela asked. Gloria nodded as she looked over the perfectly groomed course. The couples joined the group of golfers gathering in the club house.

The rules for the tournament were simple. Teams of four played Scramble, also known as Best Ball, with glowing golf balls. The not-so-serious game brought out the skilled unskilled players for a night of fun and fundraising for a local charity. Pole lights on the course weren't illuminated during this challenge, except for the one that lighted the path to the bar at the 19th hole. Only one ball was allowed per player. Once the ball was lost in the darkness, there was no second chance; players had to come in off the course.

"Hey, Wayne, have you ever finished a night game?" They all chuckled.

"Heck, no, why would I want to do that? I like being first at the bar." Voices in agreement chimed in all around.

"Okay, time to see how many holes we can get in before we lose the ball," Wayne said with a wink.

* * *

Laughter and conversation gradually ratcheted up as the crowd increased at the 19th Hole deck. When Jim, Gloria, Wayne and Pamela returned to the deck, everyone hailed them and had to know where they lost the ball.

"Not too bad. We got to the twelfth hole and the dang ball disappeared. We searched everywhere except up in the trees. We decided to pack it in and join the other losers." Wayne cocked his chin waiting for the blowback from the crowd of revelers. And they didn't disappoint him.

From the deck, the members and guests viewed the shadowy figures of the lucky golfers who were finishing up their game at the eighteenth hole. The tall pole light allowed the casual observers to see the path to the bar.

"Hey, who's that playing out there?" The gentleman sitting at one of the front tables on the deck pointed at the couple searching through the bushes off to the side of the fairway.

"I can't see their faces. Looks like they lost the ball. And so close to the end of the course, too." Lots of comments murmured among the players who had experienced the same frustrating situation.

Jim strained his eyes to see a man and woman searching along the bushes using their clubs to push branches and leaves out of the way to uncover the ball. The couple moved on down, poking into the brush outlining the far side of the fairway near the wooded areas. They moved farther into the darkness away from the fairway.

"Hell, they might as well call it quits. You can't see a damn thing out there," said Wayne.

"Maybe the ball is still lighted up. He can see it if it is." Pamela contradicted him.

A woman's scream from the darkness pierced through the laughter and music on the deck. A yellow glow flashed. Flames shot out of the dry brush, instantly igniting the entire area. Breezes quickly fanned it into a blazing bonfire consuming more and more vegetation.

Panic and confusion gripped the onlookers on the deck. Concerned only with helping the unlucky couple, Jim ran down the deck steps followed by men and women forcing their aging bodies to gallop toward the scene, forgetting the danger. Gathering their wits about them, Gloria, and other observers on the deck, grabbed phones and called 911.

Although Jim wanted to rescue the golfers, the heat and smoke were too intense to allow anyone close enough to save the couple from the raging fire. Jim stopped and spun around to face the crowd.

"Stay back. Stay back," Jim hollered as he batted his hands toward group. The thick smoke billowing in their direction invaded his lungs. He didn't want the followers injured. Their well-intended willingness to help might propel some to believe they were super heroes, not ordinary mortals.

The flames spread along the brush into the woods as the would-be rescuers watched in horror from a distance while the couple burned in the flames.

The shocked club members, sickened by the sight, scrambled back to the safety of the deck. The stronger ones assisted those overcome by the event they had witnessed.

Minutes later sirens sounded through the streets of Citrus Ridge. First responders arrived on the scene followed by police cars, fire engines and ambulances. In a flurry of activity, firemen streamed onto the golf course and into the surrounding area to contain the fire.

First responders and EMT's helped those who could stand and walk by holding onto them and escorting the shocked and weakened seniors to the deck. Members took over their care, allowing them to sit in the chairs and offering glasses of water.

A first responder stooped over a man overcome by smoke, lying on the grass. "Hey, we need some oxygen over here," he yelled. Using a calming tone of voice to lessen the man's anxiety, he said, "We're here. We'll take care of you." He placed a blanket over the man's shivering body and tucked it in around him.

EMT's moved with purpose to treat people suffering with sprained ankles and smoke inhalation, remaining cool as they attended to each problem.

"Just hold still, ma'am, we'll have you fixed up in no time." The EMT fashioned a sling to ease an injured shoulder.

The men and women who weren't physically injured tried to find words to communicate to the police the unspeakable disaster they had witnessed.

Chaos ensued as reporters and curious residents tried to break down the police barriers surrounding the area. The news media, like a hungry horde of wild wolves, recorded the after effects of the fire and interviewed the shocked witnesses.

Singed leaves of the palm trees overhead and burned trunks would be reminders of the horrifying event for a long time.

Later that night, slithering dark bodies slid quietly among the trash and debris abandoned on the club's deck. The three yellow stripes on the backs of each of the intruders reflected the moonlight. The twisting tracks in the sand around the deck were the only evidence of the midnight marauders.

* * *

The next afternoon Gloria heard the timer beep on her stove. She jumped up from reading her newspaper to check the cookies. She was never the Dora Domestic type, and she knew she was not a baker, but she did create some delicious recipes using the vegetables from Jim's garden. When the weather cooled off, she gave in to the urge to bake something calorie-laden and delicious.

In truth, baking helped take her mind off of the tragic event last night. She hoped Jim would come home with an explanation as to the cause of the fire. Theories circulated that one of the lighted golf balls exploded or someone threw a lighted cigarette carelessly into the bushes and it smoldered and burst into flame at that time. Gloria wondered how much sadness the snowbirds could handle. Dread and grief pervaded the light-hearted, carefree winter days.

She slid the baking sheet full of chocolate chip cookies out of the hot oven and smiled with satisfaction because the cookies were perfectly done. Figuring the minutes for baking them to that lovely golden brown without charring the bottoms of the cookies was the challenging part for her. Gloria kept a watchful eye on them and kept careful track of the time using the timer on her stove. She wrinkled her nose at the thought of past unsuccessful experiences of burned cookies, and the disappointment when she smelled the charred sweet treats.

Gloria's mind immediately recalled the charred remains after the fire. Overwhelmed with the memory of the fire and the odor that blanketed the area last night, her shaking hands nearly dropped the sheet of cookies on the floor. Luckily she hung on long enough to place them on the rack to cool. Swiping her hand across her forehead, she tried to erase the scene from of her mind.

Gloria scrubbed the cookie pans so hard she nearly removed the non-stick coating. If only she could scrub away the death and sadness that lingered in the background of her memory.

Jim pulled in the driveway. *Uh-oh!* She thought about hiding the cookies before Jim walked in. He didn't need all that sugar and fat, but there was no way she could get rid of the fresh baked cookie smell…*Well, that's all right. He needs something to distract him from the tragedies.*

The body count was up to eleven residents dead on Sunshine Boulevard. Only two were from natural causes. Mystery and anguish surrounded the unnatural cause for the deaths. Fear of the unknown gripped the residents. People wanted answers and actions taken to stop the killing of the senior citizens. When would the disaster spread to killing children?

Anger raged through the community because the authorities were tight-lipped about the investigation. The uproar over their silence expanded throughout the state. Was the lack of information about the unusual deaths because the investigators were so incompetent they couldn't discover an explanation for the cause of the deaths? News media followed up on charges of a cover-up by the police.

Perhaps the authorities didn't want to clarify a reason in case it would cause chaos in the community. But if something dangerous were here, shouldn't residents be prepared to battle it? Gloria's eyes widened with the realization.

Jim trudged through the kitchen door, ignoring the cookies completely. The somber look on his face made Gloria wish he had taken a dozen cookies and stuffed them in his mouth. Anything to lighten his burden even for a minute.

"Are you okay?" She studied his gray face as he pulled out a chair at the kitchen table and plopped into it. He ignored her question.

Resting an elbow on the table and a fist under his chin before he looked at Gloria, he said, "From the latest autopsies, the medical examiner's office found a pattern in the deaths."

Gloria sucked in a gasp. With her gaze not leaving Jim's, she sat down in the chair across from him.

He placed his arms on the table as if needing the extra support to help him go on.

"They've determined all of the victims died from snake bites."

Gloria's face creased into a frown as her mind tried to digest the idea. "So the autopsies proved that." She leaned toward Jim. "I know there are venomous snakes in Florida, usually in the swamps and woods." She waited for Jim to agree to that, but he didn't even nod his head. "I just don't get it. Snakes don't usually live near people."

Jim sat back in his chair and crossed one leg over the other. "I guess they do if there's no place else to live. And it looks like we're covering up more and more of their areas with concrete and buildings."

"Well, I've got to admit, that certainly is true," she said.

They sat in silence for a few minutes before Gloria asked, "Then explain to me about people turning yellow after the snake bites. I've never heard of such a ridiculous idea." She waved her hand to dismiss it.

"They think this is a mutant kind of aggressive snake. They can't figure out why they go after people. The authorities believe the snakes could've been responsible for the couple's death on the golf course because beating the bushes may have invaded their territory, but there's no explanation for the other victims. They were no threat to the snakes."

"But, Jim—"

He stood up from the table and walked to the desk. Picking up the day's mail, he turned around to face her. "I don't know, Gloria. I don't know what's truly happened. Let's drop it. We can't understand it."

Gloria stayed seated. She had wanted an explanation. Jim gave her one. But her mind could not wrap around such bizarre assumptions.

She studied her husband's slumped shoulders and the way he plopped down in the desk chair. Chocolate chip cookies wouldn't help him with extreme exhaustion. She couldn't help him. Would this outlandish theory help him to find peace?

* * *

In the laundry room, Gloria pulled the clothes out of the washer as she had done so many times. She threw the heavy clean towels into the dryer and added a sheet of fabric softener, her mind whirling with the possibilities of what could be done to find and kill the so-called deadly snakes that were killing her neighbors.

The light from the bulb illuminated the top shelf behind her. Concentrating on setting the timer on the dryer, she was oblivious to the light's reflection in the pairs of glowing eyes peering at her.

* * *

In the middle of the night, Gloria turned on her side and shook her sleeping husband. "Jim, wake up."

"What? Am I snoring?"

"Shh…I hear something out back. Someone's out there," she whispered. Her heart beat a syncopated rhythm of fear.

Jim sat up in the bed. He flipped on the lamp on the nightstand and tilted his head to listen with his good ear. "I don't hear a thing. It's probably that white cat that's been roaming the neighborhood. Go back to sleep."

Gloria snuggled next to her husband. She tried to comfort herself by believing it was a cat making the soft sounds in the night, but her ears were attuned to the night sounds. Was that an owl hooting? A dripping water faucet? An armadillo passing the house? Snakes sliding under her window? She gasped.

Leaning on her elbow and looking over Jim's back, she asked, "Do snakes make a noise when they move?"

"Oh, Gloria. Go to sleep. And no, snakes don't make any noise when they move." He fluffed his pillow and packed it under his head. "They just slither."

Goose bumps sprang out on her arms. She wrapped her arms across her chest to stop the shivers of fearing flying up and down her spine. Lying back down, she plastered her body against Jim's back and pulled the sheet up to her chin. Those night sounds were probably nothing she decided. Or were they something?

Gloria trudged out to the kitchen in the morning. It was only 6:30 and Jim was already on his third cup of coffee, perusing his seed catalogs. She smelled the fresh coffee and, like a zombie, headed for the coffee pot. She wasn't ready for morning yet after such a night of restless sleep and nightmares.

"Good morning, Sleeping Beauty." Jim looked up from the page of cabbage plant pictures long enough to greet her.

She heard the heat exchanger blowing warm air through the floor vents. "How cold did it get last night?"

"I had twenty-four degrees on my thermometer this morning. Good thing we covered up the plants and brought Paul's plants home. Otherwise they'd be goners by now."

"I could have sworn I heard someone out back last night. I couldn't go back to sleep after I woke you up. But you were snoring in five minutes." She sipped the creamy coffee to perk her up this morning. No decaf in the morning. She needed the caffeine.

"Alright. I'll go check out back if it makes you feel any better. I have to get that other seed catalog off my workbench anyway."

A few minutes later, Gloria jumped when Jim slammed the kitchen door shut on his return from the shed. His angry face was as red as a Michigan apple. He didn't have the seed catalog in his hand.

"Jim, there's no reason to get so upset over the seed catalog not being in the shed." She crossed her arms across her chest.

"It's more than a seed catalog missing. You did hear something last night. Somebody broke into the shed through the back door. They took all but two of Paul's plants. We must've scared them away when they saw our light go on." Jim shook his head and sighed.

"Did they take any of your tools from the shed?" Gloria pictured now empty shelves and items tossed to the floor by the thieving scoundrels.

"I don't think so. But they wrecked the back door getting in there."

"That's pretty crazy. Who wants a bunch of green plants?" Gloria looked to Jim. "Do you think they were looking to do something more? Do you think they could have broken into the house and—"

"No, honey, no. No. They couldn't break into our house. The shed is easier to get into with a pry bar. They were probably just kids playing a prank or proving how tough they are." Jim walked over to Gloria and put his arms around her and held her. His hug helped to alleviate some of her fear.

Stepping away from the comforting embrace, Jim looked directly in Gloria's eyes. "Do you remember when Brian was over to our house up north last year? He inspected all the plants around the pool?"

Gloria recalled their neighbor, the city cop, carrying his beer in his hand. He leaned over every plant pretending to inspect them to make sure Jim wasn't growing illegal marijuana. Brian was such a teaser. Gloria's eyebrows lifted high and her eyes grew large and round.

They both said together, "Marijuana?"

"Oh no, Jim. Paul is growing weed right here? I can't believe it."

Jim's face turned from a frown to a smirky smile. "Yeah. I knew that guy was always easygoing and mellow. Now I know why."

"Oh, please." Gloria couldn't help but laugh. "And we're taking care of it for him. I wonder how he'll take the news when he finds out someone stole his stash of plants."

"Well, we're in a peculiar situation. Do we turn Paul into the cops for growing pot? Or, if we don't, maybe he'll share some with us?" Gloria recognized that mischievous look on his face.

"Oh, puh-leeze. My pot head husband, eh?" Gloria giggled at the thought of Jim smoking marijuana. "Hmmm. I never have gotten an answer whenever I ask you if you smoked weed in college."

"No, you haven't."

"Well? Did you?"

Jim turned around and headed for the door. "I'm going to check to see if anything else is missing and work on that back door. I'll see you later."

Gloria stopped to pour another cup of coffee for herself, then hustled down the steps from the kitchen to the carport and made her way to the shed. She had to see the results of the break-in. Opening the front door of the windowless shed, she peered into the lighted shop. She could see through the shed where Jim was checking the damaged back door. The two pots of Paul's plants sat off to the side of the door.

"Is anything else missing?" She searched the work bench and the myriad array of shelves to discover any damage or missing tools.

"I haven't checked real thoroughly yet, but it seems nothing was touched other than the plants. They must've wanted them real bad. Just look at this door." He waved his hand holding the screwdriver toward the splintered door. "I guess I'm going to have to replace it. Whoever did this knew how to use a pry bar to break in here."

A booming megaphone voice jarred the unsuspecting couple. "This is the police. Come out of the shed, Mr. and Mrs. Hart. Come out now with your hands up."

Jim dropped his screwdriver and jumped away from the door. Gloria ran over to cling to him. What in the world was happening?

"Jim?" Tears welled up in Gloria's eyes. Her heart felt as if it were going to pound out of her chest.

The front door of the shed ripped open and two policemen stood aiming their weapons at the frightened couple. At the same time two armed policemen wielding their guns burst through the already broken back door nearly knocking the couple over.

"Put your hands up and walk this way," one policeman demanded. Gloria and Jim's arms shot up in the air, and they started moving quickly toward the carport and out onto the driveway.

"Officer, what is it? What's happening?"

"Please don't talk now, Mrs. Hart."

Escorted by the policemen, Gloria shuffled out onto the driveway holding her hands high above her head. She saw a line of police cars up and down her street. *I don't see our first responders or firemen among them, so I guess there's no emergency.* Curious neighbors stood in driveways and yards up and down the block.

"Just co-operate fully with us. Okay, lay face down on the grass." He motioned to the front yard.

"But, Officer…"

"Face down now, Mrs. Hart." Gloria saw one of the policemen train his rifle on her, so she dropped to the grass immediately, spread-eagled on the lawn next to the smiling dolphin statue and close to the bright orange gazing ball in the flower bed in the front of the house.

After searching them for weapons, Jim and Gloria were handcuffed and dragged up off the ground. A hefty detective in a rumpled brown suit coat approached them.

"So you have quite a nice set-up for your marijuana growing operation here. You probably thought you'd never be discovered in this nice, quiet retirement community, eh," he snarled.

Gloria couldn't take her eyes off the fleshy faced man with the yellow-stained buck teeth. "I'd like to see some identification, sir." Chin raised, she stared at him while he pulled his badge and ID from the inside of his suit coat. "I'm Detective Simons and I have lots of questions for you two."

"We aren't growing marijuana." Jim stepped between his wife and the detective. "You've jumped to the wrong conclusion, Detective."

"Okay, if you say so, but the Sergeant tells me there are marijuana plants in your shed." The detective turned to the Sergeant. "Get those plants and take them back to headquarters. They're evidence in this case."

"Detective, those are not really our—," Jim was interrupted by a commotion on the street.

"Hey, get that lady, Greg!" Policemen were yelling at each other to catch an old, skinny woman who was shuffle-walking toward the detective.

"You shut the hell up and leave me alone. I've got to talk to them." Gloria looked up to see Ethel breaking through the line of flabbergasted policemen and making her way up the driveway.

"Now listen to me. Hell, these people aren't criminals. Does this man look like a pot head to you? They're the kindest, most thoughtful people in the world." Ethel continued shouting as she approached the detective.

"Gloria here stayed with me when I fell in the bathtub. They even took in my dog when I was in the hospital." She stopped to take a deep breath as she stood on the driveway, bath robe whipping in the breeze. "They help out all the neighbors. They're watching over our neighbor Paul's house and plants right now. In fact, they even moved some of Paul's plants into their shed so they wouldn't freeze. Didn't you, Jim?"

"Well, yes, Ethel. We did. Thank you." Jim answered. Gloria was never so happy to see Ethel as right now.

"So you're saying these plants are not your property?"

"Sir, if you would just give us a chance to explain." Jim held out his handcuffed hands.

"Alright. But you'd better explain downtown at the station, not in front of all your neighbors." The detective turned to his officers. "Take them in for questioning now."

* * *

That afternoon Gloria tapped on Ethel's back door. The old woman's eyes lit up when she opened the door to let her in to her tidy kitchen. Ethel pulled out the kitchen chair for Gloria to take a seat at the table where the fresh violet bloomed in all its purple glory.

"I just wanted to come over and say thank you for coming to our defense this morning. You were very brave to stand up to the detective." Gloria smiled at Ethel and grasped her bony hand.

"Well, fill me in on how this all happened anyway." Gloria noticed her faded blue eyes sparkled with intrigue as she lowered herself slowly to the chair. "Dammit, Buttons, quiet down. He gets so excited when company comes."

Gloria pulled a chair away from the table and sat across from Ethel. "The Security Patrol in the community and the county police have been watching this teen-age boy. He lives in the park with his grandparents. Residents have reported him out late at night and being in neighborhoods not even close to his grandparents' home.

"Evidently last night, when he broke into our shed, Security was watching and called the police. As soon as he got home with the marijuana plants in his wagon, the cops nailed him and a couple of friends red-handed. They were scared and confessed to stealing and breaking in to our place. That led to the cops believing we were growing the pot and so forth." Gloria pushed her bangs to the side of her forehead.

"The boys had their eyes on those plants for awhile waiting for them to be the right stage to harvest. When he saw us moving the plants, he thought we were going to use them. So they decided they had to grab them now or lose them." Both women chuckled.

"The cops were very apologetic, but I have never been so humiliated in front of the neighbors." Gloria couldn't continue as the tears filled her eyes.

"I knew those S.O.B.s were on the wrong track." Ethel reached across the table and patted

Gloria's hand. "But what about Paul and Barb? What will happen to them?"

"The authorities notified the cruise line and had them arrested. They'll be confined to the jail cell on the ship and the police will be there when they disembark. I'm not sure what will happen to them then."

"So you're in the clear now? You and Jim won't be going to jail, will you?" Ethel's concerned expression made Gloria smile.

"Oh, no. Thanks to you. You were our witness that we were only taking care of the plants for Paul. Being a good neighbor is not illegal." Gloria snickered. "When Detective Parker heard we were at police headquarters, he came over and vouched for us. That pretty much sealed the deal for the Get Out of Jail Card."

"Well, I'm glad I could help you out. You've certainly helped me many times." She pulled a hankie from her pocket, slipped her hand under her glasses and wiped her eyes.

"We're happy to help." Gloria felt Buttons jump up on her lap. She couldn't help but scratch him behind his ears. "Anytime, Ethel, anytime. We're neighbors, you know. Thank you for vouching for us."

Chapter Eight

The next evening, Pamela lay in Noel's arms with the tousled sheets pulled over their naked bodies. A smile of pride crossed her face as she stretched her arms over her head and let the sheet slip down to reveal her breasts. Her body might be aging, but she still enjoyed a fun and satisfying "roll in the hay" in bed with her lover.

With the dim light from the table lamp on her nightstand in her bedroom, she gazed at him sleeping peacefully next to her. Thank goodness for Viagra to prolong the pleasure. She chuckled to herself. He was a gentle, considerate man and a powerful, creative lover. She never imagined she would respond to him so passionately.

Perhaps the secret tryst added to the electricity of the evening. They had plenty of time to enjoy each other while Wayne went to a computer club meeting, and Noel's wife, Rosemary, attended one of her church meetings. Pulling the sheet over her and clutching it to her breasts, she had to admit keeping their affair secret from their mates and friends only added to the elation of their new found relationship.

Pamela rolled over on her side and watched his chest rhythmically rise and fall with his even breaths. She gently brushed a long shock of silver hair away from his forehead. Did she love him or was it lust?

She didn't want to think of it as their new love, because it wasn't love that brought them together. Instead, she had intentionally lasered in on Noel as her target for romance over a year ago. His good looks and sense of humor, as well as that dazzling smile, attracted her.

She had flirted with lots of men during her thirty-five years of marriage, but never strayed from her vows, even in her later years of marriage when Wayne and she had more of a brother and sister relationship instead of husband and wife.

Always aware of men watching her when she entered the room or laughing too much at her witty charm, Pamela knew she could have any man she wanted.

Pamela nurtured Noel so that he was drawn into her scheming web of manipulation, always making it a point to catch his gaze with her seductive smile. Paying rapt attention to every word he said and agreeing wholeheartedly with him on every issue. Staying close to him so he could breathe in her flowery fragrance whenever the four of them were together. "Accidentally" brushing her breasts against him or leaving her hand longer on his thigh when she sat next to him.

She had decided he was the one who would take her to bed and break the drought of celibacy for her. With every wily feminine move, gesture, laugh, she easily captured him in her trap.

She'd decided last winter she would have sex or die. Wayne had no desire for it anymore. He wouldn't consider trying Viagra or taking testosterone shots. A few years ago, he had experienced a heart attack and had three stents implanted to open the arteries to his heart. Wayne was afraid if he had sex, he would die due to the strain on his heart.

She remembered the final conversation they'd had about sex. "The doctor said you're healthy. You're strong and well now," Pamela argued. Her arms akimbo as she stood in the middle of their bedroom.

"No, Pamela, I've told you a hundred times, no. I don't want the ambulance coming to pick up my dead body and everyone twittering about how I died having sex with you." His eyes flashed daggers at her. He threw back the comforter and pulled down the sheets. "I don't want to discuss it anymore."

Pamela moved around the bed trying to get him to at least look at her. She stopped in front of her husband, then in a slow sexy dance, she slipped off her lacy black robe revealing the matching lingerie she had purchased that morning in order to seduce him.

"Come on, honey. Talk dirty to me." She began sliding the bra strap down her arm hoping to entice Wayne to tweak her boobs or slap her on the butt like he used to do. "I want you," she said in a husky voice.

He sat down heavily on the bed without glancing at her. He laid down and jerked the sheet over him. "Stop it," he said.

Rolling over on his side, he turned his back to her and mumbled sleepily, "I'm moving to the guestroom tomorrow night."

Her stomach lurched. This would be the last time he rejected her. She marched out of the room and slammed the bedroom door shut.

Without Wayne actually voicing it, she finally got the message. Their intimate life together was over. Eventually she accepted the rejection and the new sleeping arrangements. In fact, she discovered how much his snoring had kept her awake for years.

Prowling the bars for men wasn't her style. She was considered a cougar at her age, but the young men came from a different era she didn't understand. She really wasn't interested in their music, their technology, or even in their one-night-stand attitude. Pamela didn't want to take chances with someone she knew nothing about.

So Noel was the best candidate to seduce and she set about that winter to make him know she was available. Pamela flirted with him, and he played along. It was fun to sneak secret smiles and touches when their spouses weren't watching.

She remembered the night at the 19th Hole Bar when she and Wayne met up with Noel and Pamela.

"Hey, Pamela. Really good to see you," he said as if he hadn't seen her at bowling yesterday afternoon. His brows bounced up and down several times when he flashed that sexy smile.

"Good to see you too, Noel." She hugged him tightly around his neck and ground her body into his crotch, feeling his hardness growing in his golf shorts. She grinned. Yes, he was ready.

She looked for Wayne, but he was already off to the bar and Rosemary was in deep conversation with a quilting friend.

Pamela grabbed his hand and led him over to the corner booth in the back of the large room. He followed her with no objection and scooted into the booth. She begrudgingly sat across from him. She wanted to sit close to him, to snuggle up to him. Her body was screaming to be satisfied. Yet here, in front of their spouses and the crowd of members and friends in the community, she resisted reaching across the table to touch his hand.

Her sultry eyes focused in on his lips. Because Noel had confided to her that his eight-year marriage had lost all the fun and sizzle, she felt sure this was the time to make a move on him. She yearned to be held in a man's strong arms and to share intimate moments with a man. She needed the explosion of joy and release he could provide. A sly smile glided across her lips. This had to be the right time.

Pamela had to be quick before their spouses came back. She crossed her arms on the table and leaned toward Noel. In a velvety voice she said, "I want more than a hug."

Noel's mouth curved up into an impish grin. Mirroring her posture, he crossed his arms on the table and stared into her eyes. In a hoarse whisper, he replied, "I'm all yours. Name the place and time and I'll be there."

The round shape of Rosemary appeared in Pamela's peripheral vision. Pamela whispered, "Palace Motel on Bliss Rd. 3 tomorrow afternoon." Her words tumbled over each other in her haste.

He mouthed. "Okay," then covered the tell-tale smile on his lips with his hand, straightened up and moved over to make room for Rosemary as she scooted in next to Noel.

"You guys are sure in a deep discussion," Rosemary said. "Are you making plans for the upcoming fishing trip this weekend?" She blinked from one to the other.

They both answered, "Yeah."

Pamela dared not to look at Noel. She knew she wouldn't be able to contain the laugh gurgling in her throat.

* * *

Pamela looked at the clock. Wayne would be home in thirty minutes. She gently pulled back the sheets so she wouldn't disturb Noel. Oh yes, he needed his rest after that hot round of lovemaking. A smug smile lit up her face.

She entered the bathroom off the master bedroom, leaving her clothes draped over the back of the boudoir chair in the adjacent dressing room. She closed the door, allowing only the moonlight shining through the window to light her way.

She didn't really like to see her naked aging body, but when she closed the bathroom door, her reflection in the mirror greeted her. Sliding her hands across her breasts and then placing a hand on each hip, she twisted her upper body from side to side as she inspected her curves with a satisfied grin. Even if time had allowed her body to go south, it still looked pretty good. And the years hadn't taken away the joy of sex. In fact, the years of experience actually allowed her to enjoy it more. Or did weed and wine make it even better? She muffled her wicked laugh. So much fun.

Turning on the warm water in the bathtub, she placed her hand under the faucet to gauge the temperature. When it was just right, she turned the shower on at full force, ready to step in for a relaxing indulgence with the warm water raining over her body.

Before Pamela could step in, she heard Noel's moan from the bedroom. Terror clutched her throat. *Oh, Noel, please don't have a heart attack now!* She yanked open the bathroom door, and stood frozen in the doorway. The moonlight through the window added shimmer to the yellow stripes crawling across Noel's naked body. Snakes slithered over him shrouding him from head to toe.

When a blazing yellow light filled the bedroom, she slammed the bathroom door shut. The animal instinct to escape kicked in. Clambering onto the toilet and stepping onto the granite counter, she yanked the screen off the bathroom window and dove head first into the cool night air. She landed face down on top of the flowers in the wood-chipped flower bed below. Pamela's screams pierced the night as she lay naked among the geraniums unable to run away from the gleaming snakes she feared would soon be on top of her too.

* * *

Neighbors streamed out of their houses when they heard the shrieks coming from Pamela's yard. Some carried brooms; some lugged shotguns and hand guns while others wielded knives of varying size.

Alice and Fred from next door ran across the side yard that was barely wide enough to fit a golf cart. Alice clutched a fleece blanket to her chest. They approached Pamela, gently turning her over on her back and covered her naked body with the blanket. Pamela said nothing, her eyes like those of a terrified wild animal.

Alice talked quietly as if talking to a child. "You're going to be okay. Fred and I will help you get up." Pamela's strength evaporated. Her mind was empty of any thoughts or feelings.

Alice and Fred stood on either side of Pamela, then lifted her body to an upright position. She was as limp as the flags on the golf course on a windy day. Pulling her arm around his neck and her other arm around her waist, he dragged her toward their home. The crowd of whispering bystanders fell silent as they separated to make a pathway leading through the side yard.

"Do you need help?" a man near Fred asked. Fred shook his head. "No, just stay out of the way. We're taking her to our Florida room." They continued on toward the house. "Somebody call 911," he yelled over his shoulder to the group. Immediately cell phones blinked on in unison as people hauled out their phones and called.

Another man ran to open the door and held it as they lifted her up the steps and into the safety of the room.

Pamela, in a daze, allowed Alice to take charge. She and her husband eased Pamela down so she could lie on her back on the floral couch. Alice placed a throw pillow under her head and tucked another blanket around her, but Pamela didn't stop shivering.

Silent tears slid down Pamela's cheeks. She took a deep shuddering breath and babbled. "Noel, snakes, bright yellow, cold."

* * *

Jim arrived on the scene within a few minutes after the calls. He stooped over Pamela, staring into her vacant eyes. His heart nearly stopped beating when he saw the distress she was in. He swallowed hard and reminded himself he was responding to an emergency. He had to draw upon all the skills he had learned in his first responders classes to help her as a patient. He steeled his mindset against allowing the fact they were friends cloud his judgement.

"Pamela, it's Jim. Where are you hurting?" He shook her gently, then more forcefully. "Where's Wayne? Is he in the house too?" Pamela gave him no answer and no expression.

Kneeling on one knee, he smoothed strands of hair away from her face, then squeezed her shoulder. Alice handed him another blanket which he tucked around her trembling body.

He turned to Ron who was just a step behind him. "Go ahead and take her vitals. I've got to find Wayne."

Jim squeezed Pamela's shoulder. "Pamela, you're going to be okay. You're safe here. We'll help you."

A gaggle of neighbors remained outside craning their necks and standing on tiptoes to see the woman in the Florida room.

Jim stood up and called out the open windows to the onlookers. "Did anybody find Wayne? Is he in the house?" A cacophony of voices yelled for Wayne.

A man's voice responded from somewhere in the crowd. "A couple of the men tried to get in the house, but the doors are locked. Wayne must not be home. His car's gone."

"Well, bust down the door. See what happened in there!" Jim shouted. His face flushed red with anger. The curious onlookers were not any help in the situation.

His mind raced with worry about Pamela and Wayne. Something catastrophic had to have happened to them to cause Pamela's state of shock. He took a deep breath to try and calm his roiling stomach, as well as clear his head.

Jim returned to Pamela's side while Ron checked Pamela's vital signs.

A voice from inside Pamela's house yelled through the window, "Oh, my God! Jim! Jim, it's Noel in here. He's lying in the bed. Come quick!" A loud gasp arose from the spectators.

Jim's head snapped up. Noel? His eyes widened in disbelief. He shot up from his kneeling position and stood, paralyzed with the shock of the news. The crowd's hushed whispers filled the air. Sirens sounded close by.

Thank God, the ambulance is on the way. Jim raced toward Pamela's home to check on Noel. He blocked the thoughts of Noel possibly dead in Pamela's bed. The surge of adrenalin shot through his body to keep him running toward the reported scene, one he did not want to accept as true.

Jim pushed through the people standing in Pamela and Wayne's carport. "Get away," he screamed at them. "There might be something dangerous here. Get out now!" The people scattered away from the home and re-gathered across the street. He entered the home and told the guys inside to leave. He didn't want to deal with more deaths.

Jim's heart clattered in his chest. Gathering strength to enter the room, he dreaded finding the body of his friend, Noel. As he made his way down the hallway to the bedroom, the acrid odor nearly knocked him over. Standing in the doorway, the light in the middle of the ceiling spotlighted Noel on the left side of the bed. Bile raced into his throat as he looked at the body lying flat on the back among a tangle of sheets. Noel!

"No, no, no," Jim screamed. He grasped the door casing to hold him up.

The body's extremities were yellow like the other bodies he had seen. He stumbled into the bedroom, praying his legs would hold him up.

Trails of grass and leaves from the closet covered the carpeted floor and wound up on the bed and across his friend's body. He rushed to Noel's side and felt his neck for a pulse. "Please, please be alive," he pleaded. Tears sprang in his eyes. Of course there was no pulse.

Feeling weak with emotion, Jim turned away from the ghastly sight and staggered through the house to the outside. Reaching the driveway, he bent over with his hands on his knees, gasping for fresh air. Ron and more first responders held him up, and he let them.

"Take it easy, Jim, we've got ya'," Ron said. His breathing becoming more even, Jim choked out, "Noel's dead."

* * *

"Jim, go on home. There's nothing you can do here." Detective Parker said peering into Jim's sorrowful eyes. They stood together by a police squad car. "We're combing the grounds now to see if we can find snakes or any evidence to nail down what killed your friend."

Jim faced the detective. "They exist. I'm telling you. Witnesses heard Pamela say snakes. She saw snakes on Noel's body." Jim's voice louder with each word.

"Hey, go home, will you? We can do this. We'll look through every nook and cranny and talk to every neighbor in the area." The detective placed his hands on Jim's shoulders and held him an arm's length away from him. "We can handle it. Okay?"

"I know I should go. I imagine Gloria's wondering where I am by now. She must've heard about Noel and Pamela. She was at choir practice when I left." His voice cracked.

Not only was his friend dead and Pamela in shock and injured, but the situation in which he found them was unfathomable. How would their spouses, Wayne and Rosemary, cope with the news of Noel's death? The revelation of Noel and Pamela's affair? His shoulders slumped as the weight of the truth washed over him.

99

"Royce thinks he'll get new clues about the cause of death since Noel hadn't been dead long. Now if we can just find one of those damn snakes," Parker moved his arms to his side.

Jim ran the palm of his hand across the length of his face. "Why didn't the snakes go after Pamela?"

"It looks like she was in the bathroom and not in the bed with Noel when he was attacked. The shower was still running when we went in. Neighbors told us she climbed out the bathroom window. The snakes were too busy feeding on Noel to chase her, I guess." Parker stopped talking and glanced down at his feet before looking back at Jim.

"I'm sorry. Go home, please. Gloria'll be worried about you." The burly detective escorted him to his car.

Jim didn't want to reveal tonight's events to Gloria. He couldn't face sharing the sadness and shock with her. As he searched his pockets for the keys to the car, the pungent odor of burned flesh wafted in the breeze and rattled his senses. He shook his head trying to clear his mind of the pictures of Noel dead in the bed and of Pamela, frightened and incoherent. Learning about the secret relationship between Noel and Pamela blew him away. Too much, too much for a person to comprehend.

He inserted the key into the ignition, and then dropped his hands in his lap. How would he tell Gloria about Noel's death by snakes, Pamela in a psychotic state, and the revelation about their friends' affair? The idea of breaking her heart with this news sent his stomach churning.

He pushed his back into the car seat and let the emotion flood his body. Tears spilled from his eyes. He grabbed his handkerchief out of his back pocket to swab the tears away from his cheeks and chin and wipe his nose. He hadn't sobbed like that since his dog died when he was a kid.

After taking a few moments to gather his strength, Jim placed the wet handkerchief back in his pocket. He sat up tall, started the motor and allowed the car to move forward slowly. Making his way through the crowds of curious onlookers and around the throngs of emergency medical personnel and the police who were investigating the scene helped to distract him for a few moments from the horrible night's experience. As he broke through to turn on to his route home, dread over what other deaths and loss might happen in his beloved community overcame him. But the thought banging in his brain was the sense of helplessness to stop it. When will this killing end?

Chapter Nine

That evening, Jim and Gloria settled back in their recliners. He pressed the power button on the TV remote to turn on the eleven o'clock news, dreading how the news media would sensationalize the events of the day in Citrus Ridge. In order to stay in business, entertaining stories have to keep the viewers' attention to achieve high ratings which in turn attracts advertisers. As long as viewers tuned in to find out more about the mysterious deaths in Citrus Ridge, the station would keep the story of the mounting deaths in Citrus Ridge going.

The screen flashed on with the familiar face of the polished news anchorman, Skyler. His usual dazzling smile was replaced with a sober expression tonight. "And now we turn to the retirement community of Citrus Ridge. Another person has been found dead from an unexplained cause in this senior retirement settlement. Heather Blake is on the scene."

From his expansive desk on the colorful news set, Skyler leaned in toward the camera. A huge screen behind him flashed a close-up shot of the pretty reporter.

"What can you report tonight, Heather?"

"Good evening, Skyler. The police have confirmed the death of a man, but his name is not being released yet to the media. He's one more to add to the list of mysterious deaths occurring in this area. This time, however, there's an eyewitness to the scene. Our sources report a woman in the bedroom saw snakes. Officials will not comment." Heather's pretty face turned into a frown. "Now, back to you in the studio. This is Heather Blake at Citrus Ridge Community."

"Heather, thank you. Do they know what kind or size of snake invaded the bedroom of this home?"

"At this time, we don't have that information, Skyler."

"I've always heard snakes don't attack unless they're cornered. Was the witness trying to kill the snakes?"

"Well." Heather hesitated before voicing the information. "After talking with neighbors here, it seems the man and woman were having a rendezvous when the man was attacked. He was not, or could not have been, aggressive toward the snakes. I'll have an update at 11."

"Thank you, Heather. That is troubling news. Coming up, we will find out more about these man-killing snakes from Professor Raymond Small. Stay with us."

Jim hit the mute button on the remote control so he didn't have to listen to the commercials. "Man-killing snakes. Unknown cause. It makes me sick how they blow up the story and make people scared to come out of their homes. As if snakes are waiting at their back door to attack them." Jim got up from his recliner.

"I'm getting a glass of water. You want anything while I'm up?"

"Yes. I wish you'd bring me a way to make this day go away," Gloria answered.

Jim returned with a large glass of water, eased back down into his recliner and clicked the button to unmute the audio. He was just in time to see the TV news anchor flash his blinding smile to the camera.

"We have a snake specialist, a herpetologist, Dr. Raymond Small, professor at the University of South Florida, who can provide us with information and explanation about this unusual occurrence." A skinny young man in a khaki shirt sat next to the anchor. His large horn-rimmed glasses reflected the studio lights.

"Thank you for coming, Dr. Small."

"Thank you for having me."

"Have you any explanation as to why these snakes are in this residential area?"

Ignoring the camera, the doctor looked directly at the anchorman. "Certainly, Skyler. Houses and strip malls are taking up much of the wild forest area, streams, and swamps that are home to wild creatures. The more we encroach on their environment, the more they are forced to live among humans."

"Yellow-striped snakes are reportedly attacking people. Are you aware of this type of snake living in Florida?"

Dr. Small pushed his glasses up on his nose before answering. "I need more information and a description of the creature before I can presume to name the species of the snake."

Skyler nodded his head and studied his tablet on the desk. "Why are they attacking seemingly unaware victims who pose no danger to the snakes?"

The doctor, appearing more comfortable, ventured a look at the camera. "This snake may be diseased. Perhaps the tongue, which collects scent data, is giving the snake altered information. You see, snakes sense odors through an organ located on the roof of their mouths. If something has gone haywire with that sensing organ, the animal will be confused and not able to process his habitat correctly. Their eyesight is poor, so snakes depend on shapes, colors, scent, movement, and vibrations to understand their habitat."

Skyler leaned toward the professor. "In other words, you believe the snake was sick and confused and went on the offensive?"

"Well, I can't say unequivocally that's what happened since I wasn't there, but being this aggressive is unusual behavior for a snake." He pushed his glasses back up on his nose.

"So if these snakes are acting in such a strange manner, what do you suggest we do to protect ourselves?" The voice of the news anchor squeaked with this question.

"There's not much we can do until we know the reason for the cause of the attacks and the species doing it. We don't want to go out and kill every snake in Florida, Skyler."

"Doctor, these snakes are invading our homes and killing helpless people who are not attacking them. From what I understand, death is instantaneous so there's no time to call for help or to get treatment. Shouldn't we take action now?"

"Please, Skyler, I told you we need more information—"

The newsman interrupted the scientist. "Thank you, Dr. Raymond Small." Then he faced the camera. "That's all the time we have. We'll be back after these messages for a wrap up of the day's events."

"Turn it off. I'm sick of hearing it." Gloria placed her hands over her ears. "Why did he cut the professor off like that? He had more to share."

"I'd like to have learned how to protect ourselves from these snakes. Perhaps Skyler wanted to keep the information to reveal in tomorrow's 'breaking news' segment." He placed finger quotes around breaking news.

Jim switched off the TV and threw the remote on the end table. The deaths kept mounting, but there was no way to stop them. And why were they occurring only in Citrus Ridge? Jim was frustrated with the little amount of progress made in the investigation. He wanted answers for a solution to quell the fear and anxiety overwhelming his community. He wanted the horror to stop now!

* * *

The next afternoon, Gloria parked her Buick along the curb in front of Rosemary's house. She expected lots of cars and people at the house, but only Wayne's white Jeep sat in the driveway. She remained seated after the motor cut off. Gloria dreaded walking into the house, afraid she might find Rosemary in a deep depression or perhaps in shock. Maybe it was too soon for Rosemary to feel like having visitors. She sighed. Perhaps she shouldn't bother her and yet, Rosemary might need a friend to lean on.

She had no idea what to say to Rosemary. The situation called for much more than the usual topic of weather. *Hasn't the weather been perfect? I hear it's supposed to get cloudy and cool this afternoon. Maybe we can get a little rain from it. How are you feeling now that your husband is dead, and you discovered he was having an affair with your best friend?*

Gloria removed the keys from the ignition and dropped them in her purse. She got out of the driver's seat, adjusted the purse strap on her shoulder, and opened the rear door. Retrieving the hot pads from the back seat, she leaned over and picked up the casserole dish next to them, grasping it first one way and then another. She set it back down on the seat and pressed the foil tighter over the top. *Oh, Gloria, quit fussing and delaying. Get it over with. You have to face Rosemary.*

She grabbed the very warm casserole dish with her hot pads and carried it up to Rosemary's door. As she stood on the step trying to decide how to balance the dish and ring the doorbell, Rosemary opened the door.

"Hi, hon. I wanted to drop this off for you. I won't stay. You probably don't feel like company?" Gloria's words banged into each other due to her nervousness.

"Oh, Gloria, please come in. Thank you for coming over. You didn't need to bring anything. Thank you for being so kind," Rosemary gushed. Her blue eyes seemed brighter, her hair and make-up done perfectly, and she was dressed in her crisp blue golf shirt and white Capris. She looked ready to play golf rather than plan a funeral.

Gloria was relieved to see her friend wasn't laid out on the couch in despair after discovering her husband was dead and that he had cheated on her. In fact, Gloria was a bit taken aback at her cheeriness.

Rosemary set the casserole dish on the kitchen counter then turned back to Gloria and gave her a warm hug. Gloria's eyes misted over as she clung to her friend.

Coming from the back of the house, Wayne entered the kitchen just as robust and happy as

Rosemary. He wrapped his arms around Gloria and pressed her hard against him, practically squashing her bosom into his chest. He held her tightly for what seemed like forever.

"I am so sorry. I am so sorry." Gloria's eyes prickled with tears as she tried to express herself. She didn't know if she cried because Noel was dead or that her friends had learned their partners betrayed them. *Is discovering your spouse sneaking around behind your back worse than a sudden, horrendous death?*

"Please, come in and sit with us." Rosemary led her to the beach-themed couch and motioned for her to take a seat. She sat on the cushion and pressed her back against the fish and sea shells pattern. Rosemary's colorful needlework, paintings, and handcrafted quilts brightened the small room. Rosemary sat next to Gloria and Wayne eased in to Noel's leather recliner and faced the ladies.

The silence was thick as sea fog. Gloria wasn't sure how to begin the conversation. "Have you made funeral arrangements yet?" she asked.

"No, we haven't, because we don't know when they'll release Noel's body." Wayne answered matter-of-factly.

"Oh, Wayne, I'm so glad you're here to help Rosemary." She patted Rosemary's shoulder wishing she could mend her broken heart. "If there's anything I can do, please let me know."

Looking at Wayne, she quietly asked, "Where's Pamela?"

"She's under a psychiatrist's care at the hospital. Our daughter is coming down to get her and take her home so Pamela can stay with her. I can't stand to even be near her." He grasped the arms of the recliner tightly. "My daughter is siding with Pamela."

"Siding with Pamela? You mean caring for Pamela, don't you? I'm sure you're hurt by discovering she and Noel were having an affair."

"Well, you see—" Rosemary hesitated and flicked her eyes to Wayne. He nodded. Focusing back to Gloria, she said, "When his daughter discovered her mom was seeing Noel she was very angry with her. So we had to tell her—" Rosemary licked her lips, then the words poured out of her mouth. "Wayne and I have been together for two winters. We were waiting for the right time to tell our kids, but fate made the decision for us." Rosemary glanced away from Gloria and pulled a white tissue from her pocket and dabbed her teary eyes.

Time stopped for Gloria to digest this new bombshell. Surely she must have misunderstood. "Excuse me?"

"Oh, Gloria, I'm so sorry you had to hear about us like this. Wayne and I love each other so much. Please forgive us." Rosemary's round face twisted in agony.

"Wait a minute." Cringing away from Rosemary, she asked, "Are you telling me you two are having an affair just like Noel and Pamela?" *Please tell me these dear friends are not a swinging foursome.*

Rosemary caught Gloria's gaze and held it as she twisted the wadded tissue in her hands. "We knew it was wrong, but we were attracted to each other. We refused to settle anymore for loveless marriages and a future of misery. We couldn't live without each other."

The passionate words faded into another deep silence. Gloria's eyebrows lowered and knitted together. She was so flummoxed by Rosemary's heartfelt words; she didn't know how to react to this surprising disclosure. What is the socially acceptable way to acknowledge a friend's affair?

"Did you do it just to get back at Pamela and Noel for their affair?" Gloria spat out the words. She was disgusted with them—with all four of them.

"Oh, no. It wasn't like that." Rosemary moved closer to Gloria. "We weren't aware they were seeing each other. I guess they were good at keeping secrets, like us. We've been very careful. Didn't you think I attended a lot of church meetings?" Rosemary giggled like a thirteen-year-old girl. Her eyes sparkled when she glanced over at Wayne. He returned a sly smile in her direction.

The lighthearted quip didn't seem to Gloria to be appropriate at the moment. She straightened her back against the stingray design.

"It wasn't exactly a shock when we found out about Noel and Pamela. You know, the four of us spent a lot of time together, and we always loved being together. It just seemed natural that we drifted toward the other spouse. I don't know. It's hard to explain. You have to experience it yourself."

Gloria clamped her mouth shut, knowing that was never a plan for her life. She had to get out of here before she said something she shouldn't.

Rosemary and Wayne exchanged smiles. Wayne gazed lovingly at Rosemary. His mop of white hair and short white beard framed his face emphasizing his twinkling green eyes. He seemed to sparkle when he looked at her. Gloria shifted uncomfortably on the too soft couch.

"I understand this is a lot to take in." Rosemary touched Gloria's arm. "We're devastated about Noel's death and with Pamela's state of mind. The doctor told us she may never be sane again after seeing what happened to Noel." Tears glistened in Rosemary's eyes. She took a deep breath before continuing.

"We're just glad we have each other to get us through this difficult time, and we'll get through it together. We'll come out on the other side happy because we're doing what is right for Noel and Pamela. Then we'll have the rest of our lives together." This time, Rosemary patted Gloria's shoulder.

Chapter Ten

Pamela lay in the cool blue sheets of the hospital bed curled into a ball to protect herself from the snake attacks. Who was she kidding? Nothing would stop the monsters. She gasped for breath and squeezed her eyes closed. Nothing erased the memory of helpless Noel smothered by snakes swarming all over him. She shivered as she remembered standing naked in the bathroom, but she couldn't remember how she ended up at her neighbor's house. And how did she get *here?*

Uncurling her body, she pushed herself up on her elbows and peered around the sterile room. No corner of the room or static shadow escaped her survey to find the serpents before they attacked her again. Exhausted, she fell back on the bed and pulled the sheets tightly around her as if the sheets could shield her from the snakes.

People constantly came into the room to check her, but they never stayed. Tears flooded her eyes when she realized she was alone again. No one to save her from the snakes if someone wasn't right by her side. The snakes might show up here any minute.

Pamela crossed her arms across her face. She wanted to run, to escape, but her legs felt like slabs of concrete and her whole body was about as strong as bowl full of gelatin. She wanted to go to sleep, a deep sleep, but if she went to sleep, the snakes would crawl all over her and kill her just like they did Noel. She shuddered.

Pamela closed her eyes, then snapped them open. She had to stay awake to watch for the slimy killers and scream for help. But would those people come in time to save her?

Where was Wayne? Why wasn't he here with her? He'd save her from those creatures. He always protected her and spoiled her. Fear gripped her by the throat. She whimpered in agony and terror She was afraid—deathly afraid.

* * *

Jim heard the dogs barking. He opened the blinds and pushed the windows open to let in the morning breeze. He watched the animals leaping on their leashes, ready to hunt and kill snakes. The local police, the FBI, and the state vehicles lined the entire length of the street. Jim shook his head. Those yelping dogs pulling their handlers through the neighbor's yards would scare away any critters in the area.

He heard more of the barking dogs hunting through the woods outside the park. The huge moss-draped Florida oak trees, palmetto, and scrub brush must be a safe haven for the snakes. From videos on the news, bounding through the thick bushes and palms was much easier for the eager canines than for their exhausted handlers.

Jim tried to read the newspaper in the Florida room, but the dog yelps were distracting. The warm breeze flowed through the screens and cooled his body. He enjoyed wearing a T-shirt, shorts and sandals in February, but his ideal retirement home had turned from fun and friends to stress and anger. The joy he found in his refuge at Citrus Ridge had disappeared because of those damn snakes. It was enough to drive him to smoke again. He found himself slapping his breast pocket for a pack of cigarettes although he had quit ten years ago. Now the only thing in that pocket was his glasses. He slipped them out and put them on. That was better. He gave the paper another shake to try and make the page stay open.

"Have you read the paper yet?" Jim asked Gloria as she carried her iced tea to the sunroom.

"Only the front page. And that was enough. It seems that's all they can report on. I can't handle anymore news." She eased herself into the rocking chair keeping a paper napkin wrapped around the wet glass. The humidity was merciless today.

"Look at all these ads for snake traps, snake killer, and ridiculous concoctions to keep away the snakes. People are so paranoid."

"Well, I can understand how paranoid we all are. You've heard the TV commercials. They only add to the fear. They focus on the idea of death by man-eating snakes to sell more products," she said.

Jim turned the page of the paper and shook it again so it would stand up, but it was as limp as a spaghetti noodle.

Gloria pulled a tissue from her shorts' pocket and dabbed her nose. "I wonder what genius advised using mothballs around the houses to keep snakes away. The neighborhood stinks." She wrinkled her nose.

An article in the paper reported a huge demand for caulking, drywall, and plywood at the hardware stores. Residents were sealing every nook and cranny in their homes and under them. Jim snickered. *If I were still in the hardware business, I'd probably be advertising the same as they are.* It was a great way to make a buck to pay the bills. Of course, he would sell them with full disclosure that no one knew if any of the products actually delivered on the promise of keeping the houses "snake-free."

He read another article trying to convince residents to close schools because of snake invasions. The reporter argued that due to safety precautions to snake-proof their homes, the children might be more protected at home than at school. Parents were driving their children to school to avoid exposing children to possible snake attacks on their way to and from school and at bus stops. The before and after school traffic was causing accidents, injuring many children and parents. The only comforting news was no children had been attacked by snakes.

"At least we don't have kids to worry about. Thank God," he said. "So far no child has been attacked." He shook his head feeling guilty about being glad his grandchildren were safe in Michigan.

"The thought of it makes me sick. What do you even say to a kid? How do you explain what's happening?" Gloria asked, but he had no answer for her.

Jim was shocked by the controversy for and against slaughtering all the snakes in the area. Many residents were ready to kill them by feeding them a substance making them unable to reproduce. Others argued that the State of Florida would be overrun with rodents and insects if the snake population was reduced or possibly annihilated.

Letters to the editor espoused several points of view. The environmental people called for a moratorium on building new homes and shopping malls. They wanted to set aside large tracts of uninhabited land for the wild life habitats. These areas would keep creatures from invading residential areas.

The investors, developers, and construction unions said the idea was ridiculous as there would be no jobs, homes, or services available for people moving to Florida at a rate of fifty families a day. They pointed out that no new companies would consider Florida, and many already established might leave.

"You know this problem will keep people from moving to Florida or even deter tourists from coming here for vacation. They have to get this under control or it'll ruin Florida's economy," he said.

"Not only moving to Florida, but how many will actually leave Florida? Look at how many folks have left Citrus Ridge since the snake attacks began," Gloria said.

After a long discussion this week, he knew Gloria was ready to go. He wanted to pack up and go home to Michigan and be done with the whole mess too. Their plans for a fun winter in Florida had disintegrated into a nightmare of death and devastation.

Jim folded the paper and placed it on the table so Gloria could read it later.

"I'm sick of all this mess." He removed his reading glasses and placed them in his T-shirt pocket. "If you're ready to leave for home, I'll start gathering up my stuff tomorrow."

Her surprised expression exploded across her face. "What? You want to leave so soon?" She laid her tissue in her lap. "Is it because the kids called last night wanting us to come home?"

"No, no. Of course not." He recalled the worry in his daughter's voice when she told him Citrus Ridge was on the national news. Later their son called to tell them it sounded like a dangerous situation to be in and wanted them out of there.

"I explained to the kids it's just the media sensationalizing the story. I told them not to worry about us."

"Well, I don't think that's going to keep them from worrying."

"Good Lord, Gloria, you want to go, don't you?" His voice was too loud he knew. "I thought that was what you wanted." A vein pulsed in his neck.

"Of course, I want to leave, Jim. It's just that—"

"What?" He held his hands out toward Gloria. "Be honest with me. What do you want?"

Gloria took a deep breath and focused intently on Jim's face. "I've thought through the pros and cons of leaving, and I keep coming back to the fact I'm worried about our neighbors and friends. They're so frightened. So many are stressed out. I'm afraid they'll have heart attacks and breathing problems." She sat forward in her chair. "We need to keep checking on them until this snake scare calms down. There are so few first responders still here. We really need to stay."

"Well, for Pete's sake, Gloria. I thought you wanted to leave. Now it sounds like you aren't ready to go home." He ran his hands through his thinning hair.

"I just wanted to let you know how I feel. If you think we should leave, we can." After being married to Gloria for so many years, he knew she was actually saying she didn't want to go.

Although Jim was ready to head north, deep inside he also felt an obligation as co-captain of the first responders in the Citrus Ridge community to be available. His anger masked his fear and concern for his friends and neighbors. Jim knew that even if he returned to Michigan, he would worry about them; his heart would still be in Florida.

* * *

Later that morning, Jim heard a knock at the kitchen door. "Hey, Royce. Long time, no see. How about a fresh cup of coffee?" Jim was delighted to see the medical examiner, shaking his hand enthusiastically. One good result of the horrific tragedies was the bond they had developed working together.

"That sounds great. You make a pretty mean cup of coffee. Make it strong. I need a little extra energy. None of the caffeine-free stuff with no backbone." Royce grinned at Jim.

Royce sat at the dining room table while Jim scooped out the coffee from the canister and measured the water into the carafe. He quickly poured the water in the coffeemaker and punched the button to begin the brewing. The kitchen filled with the alluring aroma of coffee.

"Boy, that smells a lot better than those damn mothballs." Royce laughed. "I wonder if there are any mothballs left at Wal-Mart."

"All I know is that the prices are jumping higher every day, just like gas!"

"How's Gloria doing, Jim?"

Jim leaned against the kitchen counter. "She's trying to be brave, but it's difficult for all of us with the death toll mounting. Discovering the affairs and losing Noel and, well, you know." Jim stopped and shook his head. If he didn't know better, he'd think he was living in a bad horror novel.

"I wanted to check in with you. You've been a lot of help to all of us trying to put the pieces together. Are you planning to go back north like most of the snowbirds?"

Jim frowned. "Hey, do you know how much snow has accumulated in Michigan? Not to mention the ridiculously cold temperatures. No way do I want to get back to that. I've spent enough winters in Michigan to last a lifetime."

"Well, so far we haven't decided to evacuate the area, but I'm afraid that may be the next step. Thank God there've been no reports of snake sightings in other places in the city or county. All of the deaths have occurred here on Sunshine Boulevard. We can't make people leave their homes, but seriously, Jim, for your sake and Gloria's, you may want to consider it."

"Thanks for your concern, but we're not at that point yet. We've discussed it pretty thoroughly. Weigh deadly snakes versus snow and cold, we're still taking the snakes." Jim smiled, although the truth wasn't a joke.

"We've come up with some theories. The scientists are saying the last hurricane may have washed these snakes on shore. They're probably not Florida natives. Something in the storm must have put their systems out of whack. The species has evolved into these creatures that have never been seen before.

"From Pamela Gates description, the snakes look similar to the everyday snakes people see around their homes and gardens with the exception of three yellow stripes down their backs," Royce said.

Jim filled the mugs with the steaming coffee and carried them to the table. "Sure. I see black snakes around here and even have one under the house sometimes. I find snake skins there all the time."

Both men were quiet as they drank their coffee.

Royce leaned forward on his elbows facing Jim across the table. "We're at our wit's end. We don't know why the snakes are killing people. We assumed the victims were sick when we got the first calls, but Noel was a very healthy guy. Still vital and virile, the way I understand it." Royce bobbed his head down toward his coffee cup.

"Well, could it be they had something on their body that the snakes smelled? Maybe they all chewed Altoids or something." Jim cracked a grin knowing how much Royce liked Altoids mints.

"Oh, gosh, if that's the case, I better high tail it out of here, eh?" Royce acted like he was scared and jumped up with his coffee cup. He placed it by the sink.

Jim laughed at Royce's comical expression.

"I have to get back to the job." He caught Jim's eyes and held them. "If I were you, I would seriously consider returning to Michigan, snowy or not. Your life may depend on it. Thanks for the coffee, and say hi to Gloria for me, will you?"

"Oh sure. She'll be sorry she missed you. When this is all over, let's plan to get together for dinner."

Jim checked his watch. Gloria wasn't due back from exercise for an hour. He planned to make some headway in his workshop. He wanted to finish a nightstand for the guest room. Working with his hands and seeing the project take shape always helped him take his mind off his troubles.

He stepped into his work shop attached to Gloria's laundry room and opened the back door. Sunlight flooded through the entrance to the shed. The sun and warm breeze lifted his spirits.

He scrounged under the bench for the oak wood he had carefully selected for the table. Jim smiled as he ran his fingers across the rich wood. Turning his back to the open door, he whistled while he concentrated on the plans for the project. He selected the tools he'd need and laid them out on the work bench.

As he reached for a box of screws, Jim felt the hair on the back of his neck bristle. He turned around to check to see if someone or something was in the doorway. Catching movement out of the corner of his eye, he glanced at the baseboard. Finding nothing, he relaxed a bit.

Boy, this snake thing is driving me crazy. Shaking his head at his jumpy nerves, he selected the screws he needed.

Chapter Eleven

The next morning Jim and Gloria's coffee break was interrupted as sirens screamed and dogs barked in the distance. When the media and the county calling alert system warned residents about snakes spotted in their area, a state of panic and hysteria gripped the community. Ignoring the police barriers blocking the roads, people rushed from their homes to find safety away from the search area, but some actually raced toward the blocked off area as if attending an attraction as big as the Super Bowl.

Jim reached for his ringing phone and listened to the message.

"Do you need to leave?" Gloria sat up straight in her chair, clasping her hands tightly together in her lap. "Is there an emergency?"

"No, I guess not. That was the alert system robo call. Sounds like the sirens are clear over on the east side of the park. We can sit tight here."

"You know, after awhile, with so many supposed sightings being called in, no one will listen. Most of them aren't snakes at all. It's like that little story about the boy who cried 'Wolf' when there was no wolf," Gloria said.

When police and environmental workers were called out, they swarmed the vicinity where a sighting was reported. A sure sign the snakes were in the neighborhood was the frenzied dog barking. That signaled the animals had picked up the scent of the snakes and were thrilled with the opportunity to go in for the kill.

After a few minutes, the phone rang again. "Yeah, Ron," Jim answered. "Uh-huh. Yeah. Okay. So you've got it under control there?" Jim turned to look at Gloria's worried face and winked at her. "Okay. Thanks for calling. Take care now."

Gloria waited. "What is it, hon?"

"They cornered the deadly monsters in the brick barbecue in a back yard on Sunshine Boulevard over on the southeast corner of the park."

From a previous call out, Jim remembered the husky police officers struggling to hang onto the dogs' leashes until the plan of attack was in place. In order to be sure that every one of the snakes was annihilated, the handlers had to encircle the creatures. They could not allow even one to escape the deadly jaws of the slobbering dogs.

"Everything's fine. They got some snakes, but Ron wasn't sure if they're the mutant snakes. Cops are collecting everything now to take back to the labs for testing and examination." He picked up his cup. "Do you need a warm up for your coffee?" he asked as if life were completely normal.

Gloria's shrieks filled the small house. Jim raced into the kitchen from his workshop finding her standing in the hallway with the closet door wide open and gripping the jacket she'd planned to hang on the rod. The look of horror on her face terrified Jim. His stomach lurched. He raced to her side.

"What is it? What's wrong?"

Without turning her head, she said, "The s…s…snakes are in the closet." Still paralyzed with fear, she loosened one finger from the jacket she held in a death grip to point into the dark area.

Jim flicked on the closet light to eliminate the shadows. He needed a shovel or a baseball bat to fend off an attack, but in his panic to save his wife from the deadly creatures, he couldn't remember where either one was. He pushed her away from the entrance and grabbed a broom near the doorway of the closet. Gripping it like a warrior ready to attack, his eyes searched the floor and shelves above.

Jim turned to Gloria and shook his head. "There's nothing in here."

"Oh my Lord, Jim. They must be loose in the house!" Her eyes widened in fear.

"Where'd you see them?"

Moving next to him, she hung onto his shirtsleeve and looked into the lighted closet. "Look right down there." She motioned to the floor of the closet. The single lighted bulb illuminated the thick, black cord to her vacuum sweeper coiled up on the floor.

"Oh my God, Jim. It's the cord." She crumpled to the floor. He kneeled beside her, his arm around her shoulders, and pulled her close to him.

"Are you all right?"

Although she shook her head yes, her pale face contradicted that.

Gloria's eyes filled with tears. "I'm so sorry, Jim. I was sure they were snakes." Sobbing like a three-year-old child, her words were more like blubbering.

With his hand holding her arm and his other hand against the small of her back, he helped her to the bedroom. She curled up on the king-sized bed. Jim sat beside her handing her tissues until she cried it all out. He wanted to cry right along with her, but he tried to act strong and reassuring. Instead, he was afraid of what the stress and anxiety was doing to Gloria. And doing to him, too.

"I know this snake scare has taken a toll on us. Perhaps we should go home and get away from all of this nonsense," he said in a soothing voice.

"Oh, yes, Jim. I want to go home." She took another tissue and wiped her eyes and red nose.

"Then it's settled. We'll leave on Saturday." He lay down beside her and held her trembling body in his arms, realizing how precious this woman was to him. He breathed in her sweet fragrance and pulled her close. She relaxed and snuggled into his arms.

'I guess I'm on edge more than I thought," she admitted, her voice muffled by her face against his chest. She pulled away from him and gazed into his eyes. "Thank you for being my knight in shining armor and saving me from that cord." She giggled.

"At your service, my dear damsel in distress." His eyes filled with mischief and he hugged her even more tightly.

"I will follow you anywhere, dear sir," she said, continuing the banter.

"Right. Even if it means through snowdrifts and over icy roads in Michigan."

She was quiet as she lay in his arms. "No, I guess not. I really don't want to leave."

Raising up on one elbow, he studied her face. "You don't? Are you sure? Do you hate the winter weather that much? You'd rather stay here in the middle of this madness?"

"Well, I can't lie. I wanted to be anywhere else than here when I felt like a snake was going to eat me! But now, with you beside me, the warm sun outside, my friends who are here. At this moment, I'm sure, I really want to stay." With a sparkle of impishness in her eyes, she said, "But a girl can change her mind, right?"

The corners of his mouth twitched up into a smile. "Right." He leaned over and kissed her on the lips. She responded as he deepened the kiss.

She caressed his face with her hands. "Thank you for dashing into the danger like my prince and saving me. You were very brave."

"Aw, shucks, Missie. All in the work day of a prince, I'm sure," He grinned. "So what's on the agenda this afternoon?" he asked in a gritty voice.

With a flirty glance, she answered. "Nothing for us that I know of. Why? Do you have any ideas?"

His eyebrows waggled. "I certainly do."

* * *

After dinner, the news anchorman on the left and the reporter on the right appeared on the split screen.

"Jim, come here. I think Heather Blake is standing out by the horse shoe pit at the club house." Gloria stood back from the TV.

"There have been reports that the deadly snakes have been seen outside of the Citrus Ridge Senior Community. Is that true, Heather?"

"No, Skyler, there are no confirmed sightings of the snakes outside of this one area. Police have received numerous reports from the community, and they have and will check each sighting that is called in. But so far, when the DEP investigated, the snakes were not the deadly ones causing the deaths in this community." She clutched her microphone tightly with both hands and continued.

"According to the authorities, three bright yellow stripes running down the snake's back are the distinguishing characteristic of the mutant snakes. They're a dark, dark green, so dark the green looks black in certain lights."

"I know the police and DEP have been using dogs to catch and kill the snakes. How is that program going?"

"Right, Skyler, from all the agency's reports, the dogs have been very effective in killing the snakes. Police are taking the remains of the dead snakes back to the lab where the contents of their bellies and studies of the snake's anatomy take place. There have been no human deaths or sightings in the last week."

Jim turned to Gloria. "Who knew no deaths in one week would be something to brag about?"

They sat down in their recliners to watch the anchorman and reporter discuss the situation

"What about the dogs? Aren't they in danger of being killed by the snakes?"

"Well, so far, the police have reported no injuries to the dogs because they're quick, and they know how to keep away from a snake bite." Heather smiled into the camera. The breeze flipped her blond hair away from her face.

Jim didn't want to watch the report, but he couldn't pull himself away. He wanted to know about the danger in his neighborhood. It was like watching a NASCAR race and waiting for a crash.

"What measures are the authorities taking to insure the human-eating snakes won't return?"

"Human eating snakes? For God's sake. The news is constantly dramatizing what's happening. They're making it sound like a Hollywood horror film. The snakes are not eating anybody!" His eyes narrowed with irritation at the reporting.

"But, Jim. You know people are dying because the snakes are killing them." Gloria moved to the edge of the chair. "Isn't that horror enough?"

Jim didn't look at Gloria, staring intently at the screen where Heather was explaining plans for wiping out the mutant snake population.

"Experts have suggested introducing the mongoose which is a natural enemy. Ingested venom is harmless to a mongoose. However, there's a problem bringing them into Florida. The mongoose was imported into the West Indies to kill rats, but they destroyed most of the small, ground-living creatures. In Hawaii, the mongoose ate eggs devastating the bird population on the island. For these reasons, it's illegal to import a mongoose into the United States, even to zoos. However, there is a group heading to Tallahassee next week to try to persuade the lawmakers to repeal that law. Now from Citrus Ridge Senior Community, this is Heather Blake reporting."

The anchorman frowned. "Isn't there anything else the authorities can do?"

132

Heather's eyes widened. "The Department of Environmental Protection has indicated they will be introducing King snakes into the area this week. These are snakes that feed on snakes. We don't have much information on how this will be done, but we'll be looking into that plan. Now back to you in the studio, Skyler."

Jim wondered how Heather pasted on that smile after giving such a report about deaths and deadly snakes.

"Thank you, Heather. Stay safe."

Looking straight into the camera as if connecting with the viewers, Skyler said, "Now we turn to our resident snake specialist, Dr. Raymond Small, who is here to answer more of our viewers' questions on the situation with the deadly snakes in the region."

Turning to the man on his left, he said, "Welcome, Dr. Small."

"Thank you, Skyler." The beleaguered herpetologist faced the camera and used his middle finger to back up the heavy horn-rimmed spectacles on his nose. The thick glasses magnified the dark circles under his swollen eyes. Long days of fieldwork pushing through uninhabited regions locating snake populations and days in the lab dissecting all species of dead snakes were taking a toll on the scientist.

"Doctor, so far, the deadly snakes have been found only in the Citrus Ridge Community. Viewers have been asking about the snakes moving into different territories. What is the likelihood of that happening?"

A banner popped up near the bottom of the screen above the news crawl introducing Dr. Small as a scientist and professor at the University of South Florida.

"At this point in time, we feel the snakes haven't multiplied exponentially, which would require them to migrate to different areas. They seem to be staying in the vicinity of the senior community, but we have not discovered why. Perhaps there's a nutrient or an environment there confining them to the area."

The anchorman nodded his head.

"What can you tell us about the introduction of the King snake into this area? Are they dangerous to humans? Will they upset the eco-system here?"

"So, the King snake is native to Florida. It has not been seen in this vicinity for a while. It's not dangerous to humans unless it's cornered, but it will attack for survival."

The scientist looked away from the camera and motioned to someone out of view. "Wendy, bring that King snake here, please."

Skyler's tanned face turned white. His eyes grew wide with terror. "Oh, Dr. Small, we really don't need…"

The perky graduate student placed the caged snake on the desk in front of the squeamish anchorman. He pushed his chair away from the menacing creature curled tightly in the corner of the screened box. When Wendy reached for the latch on the door of the cage, Skyler sprang from his chair revealing his lime green golf shorts below his suitcoat and tie. "Stop!" He yelled and slammed her hand down on the desk and pulled it away from the cage.

After realizing the snake stayed in the cage, the usually unflappable anchorman sat down to catch his breath. Unfortunately, the cameraman did not follow Skyler's movements when he stood up again to wheel his desk chair back to the desk. Instead of a close-up of the newsman's face, the audience got a screen full of his crotch in his lime-green shorts.

Gloria laughed out loud at the newsman's dilemma. "I don't think that newsman would have come to save me from that so-called snake in the closet."

'"If nothing else those green shorts would frighten away a snake," Jim said.

The TV camera focused on the coiled reptile in the cage. With a nervous laugh, Skyler said, "Sorry about that. Snakes are not one of my favorite things." He smiled weakly into the camera.

Smoothing his hair back into place, he addressed the scientist. "Now Doctor, what else can you tell us about King snakes?

"King snakes use constriction to kill their prey. They eat other snakes, lizards, rodents, birds, and eggs. The "king" in their name is a reference to their ability to overpower other snakes." Doctor Small cleared his throat. "A King snake can eat even a venomous snake because the venom it ingests doesn't cause death. If the poisonous snake bit it, however, it would die."

The renowned expert relaxed as he began speaking intently on his specialized area of study. "Some species of King snake, for instance, the Scarlet King snake, are colored and patterned similar to the venomous Coral snakes."

"I recall a little childhood rhyme that helps kids remember whether a snake is deadly or not. Now how does that go?"

"Oh, yes, we teach it to children. Look at the color of the rings on a snake," Dr. Small said.

Jim perked up and recited along with the scientist. 'If red touches black, it's okay, Jack. If red touches yellow, you're a dead fellow."

"I've never heard that." Gloria said.

"Maybe you and your friends better learn it now too," he said with a grin. He turned his attention back to the doctor on the screen.

"There's another one that helps remember if a snake is poison. Red on yellow, kill a fellow. Red on black, venom lack."

"Well those are clever ways to remember. And very helpful. Thank you." Skyler smiled into the camera.

"Helpful is a good word to describe snakes," Dr. Small continued. "I want the general population to appreciate that snakes are very helpful to human beings. As we have seen with bears, coyotes, and deer, animals are displaced from their natural environments due to human encroachment. Building residences and shopping centers, pouring concrete over the land eliminates their habitat. They're forced to forage in settled areas. We must find a way to stop this land snatching so that man and nature can live together without interfering with the ecosystem. You see—"

The camera swung away from Dr. Small and focused on Skyler.

"I'm sorry but that's all the time we have. Thank you for taking time from your research to be with us, Dr. Raymond Small. Now, folks, stay with us for more news after the break." The screen flashed to a commercial for a company offering home inspections for snakes.

"Looks like he cut Dr. Small off again. Getting the commercial in is more important than broadcasting scientific information and suggestions for solving the craziness right here in our area," Jim said. "I wish the news brought some reassurance and hope to everyone that this killing could be brought to an end. We need to hear progress about some progress in eradicating these snakes."

"I have faith the authorities are working on it. I'm sure they're doing their best," Gloria replied.

The fact that perhaps there was no solution for the problem niggled in Jim's brain, but he would never suggest that to Gloria

Chapter Twelve

The next morning, Jim entered his workshop to grab a screwdriver to repair a handle on the window in their bedroom. He searched through all the clutter on his workbench, moving his drill to one side and picking up his seed catalogs to be sure the right screwdriver wasn't hidden under them. The more he searched the higher his blood pressure went and the more frustrating he became pawing through all the clutter.

Finally he picked up a screwdriver, but when he realized it wasn't the one he needed, he threw it down on his workbench in disgust. His disheveled workshop taunted him with its disorganization.

The Phillips-head screwdriver had to be in here someplace. He picked up the nail apron, looked under the garden catalogue, pushed aside the drill, and dug under the scraps of plywood. He still couldn't find the damn thing.

Jim stepped back from the table, checking the tools hanging on the pegboards, or rather the spaces where tools should be hanging. With all the craziness in the community, he had no time to complete any shop projects, let alone organize it, or care for his garden.

There was nothing else to do but start cleaning up his workshop and reorganizing it. He hoped for enough time to get at least part of it put away before he had to leave again.

The first responder calls and meetings, the neighborhood security patrol, and the overwhelming demand by several of the folks needing help and reassurance had stolen all of his free time. Someone was always stopping in at his house. He had no idea how many cups of coffee he and Gloria had shared with visitors. They had even invited Heather Blake and her crew from the local TV station in yesterday. He remembered how much Heather had appreciated their invitation to come in.

"Thanks so much for inviting us. My feet are killing me." The weary TV reporter gracefully sat down on the couch in the Florida room while her crew stayed in the kitchen with Gloria. Jim took a seat in the chair across from Heather.

She slipped off her stiletto pumps. "I'm so grateful I can wash my hands with soap and warm water in a clean bathroom. I feel so grimy trying to work and practically live out of that TV van."

Beautiful Heather sipped her coffee like it was expensive wine. Her long fingers with red manicured nails wrapped tightly around the steaming mug as if someone might snatch it from her. "This coffee is delicious. Thank you.

139

It hits the spot." She took another sip and her shoulders relaxed.

Jim grinned at Heather. She seemed so young. He realized she was probably near his daughter's age, too young to be responsible for keeping the world posted on the terrifying and dangerous situation in his community. The mutant snakes news in Citrus Ridge had elevated Heather to filing stories on the network's national news programs. Her future in broadcasting looked promising now that she was the on-the-scene network's bright and capable reporter.

"Off the record, Jim. How are you getting through all this turmoil here? So many deaths of innocent people and families and friends mourning the lives lost. It's been a difficult story to tell to our viewers. But for the sake of the public's safety, we did our best to tell the truth."

"I appreciate that very much, but the advertising and teasers were troublesome for us to watch," he said. "The relentless coverage of the story reported twenty-four hours a day seemed a little over the top."

Heather's eyes gleamed with tears. "I understand what you mean. I apologize if it was upsetting to you." She slid to the edge of the cushion. "It's a difficult situation. Our viewers were concerned about the story and the ramifications of the snakes spreading throughout the area."

Heather leaned toward Jim, a look of concern clouding her face. "Are you guys feeling less threatened now? Not quite as worried about snakes in the vicinity?"

"Well, we're feeling safer now. The police and dogs patrolling the neighborhoods and the woods give us some comfort. Most of the residents have sealed their windows and doors and filled in holes or small spaces so snakes can't enter. And the good news is there have been no deaths by snakes in the last couple of weeks." Just saying it out loud made him feel lighter.

"I've heard about some of the measures people have taken. Have you tried the glue boards?" Her perfectly groomed eyebrow arched.

Jim remembered the story she reported on making glue boards by attaching rodent glue traps or slathering a sticky substance on a board and nailing it to walls or baseboards to catch the snakes. "No, we didn't try the glue boards. We were afraid we'd catch a dog or cat instead of a snake in the glue." He loved the way Heather's blue eyes sparkled when she laughed.

Evidently the girl never got out of the inquiring reporter mode to take time to rest and relax.

"So what do you think about introducing the King snakes? Are they effective?"

"I have my doubts about a King snake being able to get rid of these killer snakes. If only we could train the Kings to hunt down the snakes and kill them like the dogs can."

He smiled at the memory of her sitting in the living room and chuckling at the idea of training King snakes. He had enjoyed visiting with her yesterday and getting to know her as a person, not as a part of the press trying to make money off other people's tragic stories.

Jim forced himself to get back to reality and faced his workbench determined to at least make a dent in the pile of stuff loaded on top of it. He switched on the two-dollar radio he'd purchased at a yard sale to the only channel it would pull in, an oldies station, and relaxed for the first time in a long time. Tidying up his workspace he hummed along to *Sittin' on the Dock of the Bay* and felt his heart slow down with the beat of the music and his shoulders relax. Perhaps life may be getting back to normal.

He set to work on the huge task ahead of him thinking about the possibility of returning to Michigan in the spring. He would be able to travel home with no worries about the friends he would leave behind. The happy thoughts brought on his full throated, loud voice to join the Beatles singing *Yellow Submarine* on the radio.

Jim opened the back door to bring in more light and a breeze. He sorted through screws, washers, and nuts and put them back into the glass baby food jars. He replaced the tools on the pegboard and smiled, realizing he saw the top of his workbench again

He whistled along to the Four Season's *Big Girls Don't Cry* while he tried to find places to stash the left over wood pieces from his finished projects. As he stooped over to pick up another board, his eyes caught a movement on the floor along the baseboard. He cautiously stepped back from the wood pile and raked his gaze across the area.

His heart raced when he spotted long yellow stripes shimmering in the sunlight streaming through the door. The stripes dazzled for an instant, and then disappeared in the dark recesses of the shop.

Oh my God!

Sweat collected in his armpits. His body tensed with the realization the snakes hid in the shadows within a few feet of where he stood. Was there one or a dozen waiting in the corner to attack him?

The kitchen door opened and shut. "Gloria, go away! Don't come in here!" he screamed at his wife. He was not going to let the snakes attack his wife.

"What is it? Are you okay?" She rushed into the laundry room and saw him through the open doorway, standing in the workshop motionless.

"I told you not to come in here," he said through clenched teeth. In a low voice, as calm as he could be, he said, "Don't make any sudden movements. Back away and call 911. There's snakes in here. I don't think they're the deadly ones." He never lied to his wife, but this was a special circumstance. He'd lie again if he knew it would make her leave.

"Oh my God, Jim. Run away! Run now!" Her voice pitched higher and higher with every word.

"I can't argue! Hurry! Call 911," he shouted. "And don't come back in here!"

Gloria turned and raced out the door. Jim thanked God at least she would be safe.

Reaching deep within his inner core, he found the strength to steady his screaming nerves and watch for the snakes. If they escaped from the work shed, they'd be gone in an instant ready to prey on an unsuspecting neighbor. He had to stay and keep them in his sight until help arrived.

Damn, if only I had put down a glue board in that corner. The thought briefly entered his head reminding him of Heather and her red nails. Would she report his death by snakes on the national news?

"No, by God! No!" Jim ripped the newly sharpened shovel off the wall beside him, pushed the table saw out of his way and in one fluid motion hacked at the corner filled with thick, long snakes.

Adrenalin pounded through his veins. He drove the shovel into the pile of deadly creatures. Chopped pieces of snakes writhed on the cement. Lidless eyes glinted in the disembodied heads as they flew through the air.

Golden liquid coated the head of the shovel and spattered onto him. Wherever the thick substance landed, his skin prickled and turned yellow, but he ignored it. He was afraid to stop. What if he missed one?

He hacked along the base of the wall taking vengeance on these snakes who killed Noel, ruined Pamela, murdered friends. He was not going to allow them to get to his wife or take more lives. Not ever again.

After chopping his way through the pile of killer snakes, his shaky legs felt like he'd run a marathon. With aching arms unable to strike at the serpents, he threw the shovel at the corner. It took all of his strength to run to the front of the shed and out into the sunshine, slamming the shed door behind him ensuring none followed him.

The sirens screamed down Sunshine Boulevard. The K-9 unit pulled in to Jim's driveway, the feverish yelps of the dogs alerting neighbors of the danger. Police poured out of the vehicles. The officer shouted instructions and motioned to the others to surround the area.

"In the workshop, in there." Jim swiveled his head toward the door. He collapsed in the grass, gulping for breath to calm the thundering heart in his chest.

"Jim, you're okay. You're safe." Ron kneeled beside him, his eyes searching for signs of injury or shock. His strong hand grasped Jim's shoulder. "We've got ya' now. Take some time to just lay there before you try to get up.

Okay, buddy?" Jim, too exhausted to reply, did as Ron suggested, thankful for his help.

"Where's Gloria?" His eyes filled with anxiety.

"The police won't allow her near here. She's fine. I saw her as I came in." Jim, using his hands under his head as a cushion, remained on his back in the cool grass. "She's okay. Then everything's okay."

Chapter Thirteen

"I'm fine, just fine." Jim stretched out in his recliner in the living room.

Gloria thought he looked comfortable but not fine. His colorless face and erratic breathing proved he wasn't completely recovered from his ordeal with the killer snakes earlier that morning. Holding his mug of coffee in both hands didn't help conceal his still trembling hands.

Gloria fussed over him to help her forget the danger he had faced in his workshop and the possible deadly consequences for Jim. She shuddered even thinking about how close he had come to death and how stupid she had been to not run and call 911 instead of arguing with him about getting away from the snakes. Or was he the stupid one? Jim stayed and slashed the snakes to death, but what if one, just one—? She moved her hand to her stomach to stop the churning at the thought of what might have been.

No doubt about it, Jim was lucky to be alive, but very foolish for putting his life in jeopardy. She smiled as she pictured him truly as her knight in shining armor, slaying the snakes and protecting her and the entire community. Hopefully, because of his actions, the death toll from snake bites would stop increasing, and no one would be called to the scene of another victim of vicious attacks by the deadly monsters.

Gloria leaned over to take the empty coffee mug from Jim. She caught the peculiar smell of his body even after he'd taken a hot shower. The medical examiner's techs had carefully scraped samples of the yellow liquid from his body and bagged his clothes to take to the lab for further examination. Evidently he needed more scraping to get that odor out of his skin.

She took the cup from him and set it on the end table beside his chair. She hated seeing him so weak and not his usual robust and happy self. He was a strong man and in good shape for his age, but this fight to the death tested his physical stamina. The struggle left him physically weakened and an emotional wreck. His outlook on life would never be the same.

Jim detested her hovering over him, but the future of his health was uncertain. She worried what would happen to his body. What about the yellow stuff on his skin? No one really knew what it was or what effect it would have on his health. The episode could leave him with permanent health problems and eventually kill him. She choked back the knot in her throat, squared her shoulders and acted positive and strong for him.

"Do you want a blanket?"

"Nah, I'm fine." Jim reached for her hand and squeezed it gently. "Really, hon, I'm okay. The docs said I'm fine." His eyes pleaded with her to believe him, but she didn't.

"Well you certainly don't look fine. We should go to the ER and get you checked again. Your color isn't good."

"Cut it out, Gloria," he said in an impatient tone of voice. He dropped her hand. "For the millionth time, I am not going to the hospital. I need to sit here for a bit longer, that's all. I told you I took care of those damn snakes before they hurt me."

"Yes, you did, honey." Gloria spoke in sweet, measured tones. An impish grin crossed her face, "But those damn snakes scared the hell out of you. I don't know if your heart can take all that excitement." Her eyes twinkled as she teased her husband in a sing-song voice trying to lighten his mood. She snickered, and his gaze met hers, resulting in the first smiles since the incident.

* * *

The next morning Gloria spotted the news people and their trucks lined up along the street. Curious neighbors stood in her yard. She shook her head in disgust. The onslaught of TV camera crews and news reporters from all over the country milled about the lawn as if it were a public park instead of their private property.

149

Yesterday, all day, friends and news people had shown up at their door after Jim's horrific nightmare with the snakes. This morning, when they knocked on the door, she cordially greeted each one after plastering a smile on her face to cover her annoyance, but she never allowed anyone in to question Jim, not even friends. He needed to rest and recuperate. A few visitors even had the audacity to peek in the windows of the Florida room.

The phone jangled in her pocket. Pulling it out, she noticed Heather Blake's phone number. She considered ignoring the call, but Heather was so persistent, she knew she'd call back again and again.

"Hello," Gloria said in a hard voice.

"Ah, good morning, Gloria. This is Heather Blake from NBC News."

Gloria sighed. Of course she knew she was from NBC News. "Hello, Heather."

"Sorry we couldn't connect yesterday. How's Jim feeling?"

"He's not doing well at all. Please don't call again. He's in no shape to talk to you or any reporters."

"Oh, I'm sorry to hear that, but…"

"Good-bye, Heather." Smiling with satisfaction at shutting down at least one story on the snake "event," Gloria clicked off the phone.

Dread washed over her when she heard a knock at the kitchen door. She couldn't bear anymore of the small talk with another neighbor who wanted to get in to see Jim. When she looked through the window, she was delighted to spot the medical examiner, Royce

"Come on in. I just made fresh coffee." She motioned him in and quickly shut the door. "Go cheer up Jim. He'll love to see you."

Royce had been a frequent visitor ever since the killer snake ordeal had begun. She had become accustomed to serving him black, strong coffee.

"Ah, coffee sounds good. Thanks." Royce said. He walked on into the living room.

Jim's face lit up when he saw his friend enter. He started to put the footrest down, but Royce said, "No, no. Don't get up." He clasped Jim's hand in both of his and shook it firmly. Gloria quickly followed with his coffee.

"How're you feeling this morning?" Royce asked. Gloria noticed his brow furrow with concern for Jim.

"Oh, I'm fine. Just fine." He bobbed his head and smiled, then skewed his eyes at Gloria. "Have a seat. Good to see you."

Gloria handed Royce his coffee after he had settled into the cushions on the couch, leaving Gloria's recliner available for her.

Royce saluted her with his cup. "Thank you. Best coffee in town." He sipped the hot brew, then set his mug on the starfish end table.

Jim's demeanor brightened as he exchanged small talk with Royce. Gloria noticed his eyes actually sparkled and his gray face colored with life.

"Royce, do you think Jim should go back to the hospital? His color isn't good this morning." Gloria was sure he would take her side.

"I'm fine." He darted a look at his wife. "I'm a little stiff from smashing that shovel into those snakes, but I feel okay."

Royce stood up. "If you don't mind, can I take a look at you?" He checked Jim's eyes and examined his arms and legs for snakebites. He studied the discoloring where the liquid splashed on his skin.

"Any fever or headaches?" Royce stepped back and studied Jim.

"No, just kind of tired after all the exertion."

"You look all right to me, but be sure to keep an eye on those spots. Don't hesitate to see a doctor if they start to burn, itch or get red. Okay?"

Gloria made a face at Jim. No, he didn't have to go to the hospital according to Royce. Jim won that disagreement.

Royce returned to his seat. "Are you up to talking about what happened yesterday? I have the police report here." He waved a manila folder in the air.

"When I arrived yesterday, you weren't in very good shape to talk to me." He pointed to his chest. "Maybe I can coax more out of you this morning?" His wily grin helped to break the serious intention of the questioning.

"If my answers can help, I'm happy to talk about it."

Royce moved up to the edge of the couch and fixed his gaze on Jim. "Thank you. Please tell me what happened and start at the beginning."

Gloria listened as Jim began explaining he was out in the shop trying to clean it up and organize it. She didn't want to relive the horrible memories, but if his story helped to explain these vicious attacks, it would be worth it.

"How close were you to the snakes when you first saw them?" Royce asked.

"I'd say about four feet away. When I grabbed the shovel and started flailing away, I was only a shovel handle away from them." Jim said. Gloria shuddered at the thought of how close he was to death.

After relating the nightmarish episode including how the yellow liquid splattered on him, Jim seemed to deflate from exhaustion. With a wave of her hand, Gloria signaled Royce to stop the interview.

"I appreciate how difficult it is for you to have to relive this every time you tell it to the investigators. I want you to know you've given us a lot of valuable information to help us put the puzzle pieces together," Royce said. "I don't know if you realize how many lives you've probably saved by destroying those monster snakes."

Looking at Gloria, Jim's chin quivered a bit from the compliment. This time she smiled with pride as she realized he was right again to stay and fight those deadly snakes.

Royce faced Gloria and asked, "How's your friend Pamela doing?"

Gloria's eyes misted over, still grieving the loss of their friendship and the person she thought she had known.

"She's made some progress and can carry on a conversation now that makes sense. She's seeing a psychologist or psychiatrist. I don't know the difference." Gloria felt uncomfortable with her ignorance. "We haven't kept in touch with her, but Rosemary told us that Pamela's recuperating at her daughter's home."

"I'm sorry. I know this has been difficult for you," Royce said. He looked from Gloria to Jim. "Thanks, ya'all. I think I'd better leave now and let you get some rest unless you or Gloria have any more questions."

Jim looked at Gloria. She dipped her head to encourage him to go ahead and ask. "So yes, we were wondering why the snakes didn't attack me while I was cleaning the shop. I would've been easy prey for them. Can you answer that?" Gloria sat back in her recliner anticipating the responses she hoped would satisfy what had kept both of them awake all night since it happened.

"We do have some theories." Royce opened the manila folder, then closed it. "I must caution you they're only theories for the moment. Things may change later. So I really can't share why I'll ask these questions. Are you okay with that?"

"Sure. I'm game. What do you want to know?" Jim grinned. Gloria always loved that gentle grin. A flood of sorrow overcame her when she realized she may have never seen that lovable expression on his face again if he had been murdered by those vicious snakes.

Royce nodded and reached into his shirt pocket for his pen and pulled a paper from the folder. Using the folder as a makeshift desk, he placed it on his knee and scribbled something at the top of the paper.

"We can move to the kitchen table so you can be more comfortable taking notes," Gloria said.

"Oh, thanks, Gloria, but I do this all the time. This is fine."

After studying the sheet of information, he looked up and said, "We have the medical history of the deceased. I'd like to compare your overall health and the medications you're taking with the victims."

Jim nodded. Gloria licked her lips, anxious to get on with the questions. She could barely wait to develop her own theories about why these creatures were ravaging their community.

"Are you taking any prescription drugs now?" Royce asked

Jim looked at Gloria. "Um, what is that pill I take for my arthritis, Gloria?"

"He takes Ibuprofen, but that's over the counter, not a prescription drug. He also takes a daily multi-vitamin for mature men." Grinning at Jim, she reached around the lamp on the table between them and lovingly tapped his arm. "Did you stop taking glucosamine?"

"Yeah. I heard all the hype on TV and tried it for a few weeks. It didn't do anything for my sore joints." Jim shook his head. "Those marketing campaigns make you believe you've got to have it, and it's the best thing since sliced bread. I've learned not to believe everything you see on TV and the Internet."

Gloria was getting impatient. Enough. She wanted Jim to answer the questions and move on.

Royce jotted down notes on the paper. Without looking up, he asked, "Are you a marijuana user?"

Jim looked at Gloria. "No, I don't need that either." His impish smile spread across his face "Nor have I ever smoked it." He winked at Gloria. After all these years of asking Jim about smoking weed, he finally answered her question. She realized it really didn't make any difference to her now. But she smiled with satisfaction that he had finally told her. She'd won that round even if it was a medical examiner who got the answer for her. And perhaps his answer would be important to the investigation.

"Are you taking anything to lower cholesterol? A statin?"

"No, my cholesterol count's great." Jim leaned toward Royce. "Why do you want to know if I'm smoking marijuana and drugs for my health?"

"Ah, Jim that's one of those questions I can't answer. Sorry. I can't take chances on revealing a theory we're working on."

Gloria's face crumpled. "I know that's what you told us. But from your questions, I'm sure the victims must have been taking marijuana and, perhaps, a statin. Is that right?"

Royce laughed. "I was afraid you'd be able to figure something out, Gloria. So I guess I'd better explain so you won't have to keep wondering and being anxious about Jim being a target of the snakes again."

"We'd really appreciate that," Gloria said. Now if only he'd explain it clearly in everyday language they could understand. She was desperate to finally comprehend what happened during this grueling time in their lives. She wanted to tell Royce to get on with it before they died of natural causes!

"This isn't really something we want to share with the public. As I said, it's only a theory and nothing proven."

Alright already, Gloria thought. She was ready to reach over and rip the folder from Royce and read the information herself.

Jim bobbed his head. "Of course, you can trust us not to reveal anything that shouldn't be made available to the public."

"Considering I've worked with you these past weeks and gotten to know you over several cups of coffee, I know I can trust y'all," Royce said.

Gloria nodded and inched to the edge of her seat. She wasn't sure if it was to hear better or to grab Royce by his tie and strangle him if he didn't tell them soon.

"Here's why I'm asking. After studying the victims' medical histories, we discovered every one of them had a history of high cholesterol controlled with a statin. Some were marijuana users, but they were all taking a statin."

Royce hesitated. Gloria waited anxiously, realizing he needed time to decide how to divulge the full story behind the deadly assaults.

Royce spoke low and quietly because the windows were open, and the walls were thinly insulated. "Many of the test results are back from the laboratories with the information we obtained from the autopsies. The victims were all in various stages of necrosis, but had the same characteristic snakebites and yellow skin. The longer the bodies lay undiscovered, the more yellowing and eventually powder-like the bones and tissue became."

Gloria squenched up her face, realizing what nightmarish scenes Jim had experienced. No wonder he couldn't sleep with such images playing through his mind. Her heart broke for him.

"Each victim had their own particular health problems, but they shared a common denominator. Every one of them took a statin to lower cholesterol in their blood. We believe that is what attracted the snakes. When using that drug, the blood and tissue of the victims, whether male or female, have a distinct scent these snakes can distinguish."

Royce's energy ramped up, and his hands punctuated every sentence as he explained the details.

"We think the snakes attacked when they smelled that particular scent from the statin medicine. Believe me, we've learned a lot about snakes in the last six weeks. They may not have good eyesight, but their sense of smell is sharp."

The doctor interviewed by the news anchorman flashed through her mind. He had said the same thing about the snake's highly-developed sense of smell.

"When the investigators checked your home, they found old skins the snakes had shed under your house. That means they had been in your vicinity for a while, and yet they never attacked you. This supports our hypothesis. You not taking the statin is why they never assaulted you." Royce glanced from Jim to Gloria and back to Jim. He picked up his cup and took a sip of the cooling coffee.

Gloria's head nearly exploded when she realized she could have been a candidate to become a feast for the snakes. "Statins? I guess I should be glad my body couldn't tolerate that medicine, huh?"

159

Gloria crossed her arms across her chest. She knew a lot of people their age and older who took cholesterol-lowering drugs on a regular basis. After Jim's close call with the serpents, thank goodness, he didn't take that medicine.

"Why, Royce, why would the snakes choose to—?" She licked her lips, wondering how to phrase the question. "I mean, why would they attack a person, especially one who is not provoking them?" she asked. Now this was personal, affecting her life. She needed to know how to protect herself.

Royce set the cup back on the table before answering. Gloria wished he would drink the dang coffee later.

"The snakes injected their venom into the victim to paralyze the body, then sucked out the blood. They needed the statin-tinged blood to survive."

Gloria felt sick, realizing what a horrible death her friends had suffered from these vampire snakes. She could have been a victim too if she had been taking that statin.

"Essentially, when feasting on the blood, the snakes extracted all the body fluids from the victim. Having no liquid in the cells, the body dried out similar to a mummy."

Gloria, stunned by the explanation, sat speechless in her chair, pushing her fist into her stomach to keep her breakfast down.

"Maybe this was too much information for you. I'm sorry if I've upset you," Royce said.

"No. No, we wanted to know," Jim said. "Are you alright, Gloria?" He put the footrest down on his recliner and started to get out of the chair.

"No, don't get up, hon. I'm okay." She inhaled deeply. "Kind of sick to my stomach, but okay," she said.

She stood up on shaky legs. "Anyone need a glass of water? I know I do." With no takers, she marched into the kitchen to fill a glass for herself, hoping to settle her stomach and give her time to absorb all of the horrifying information Royce had shared. She listened to the conversation in the living room as she stood at the kitchen sink.

"Do you have any more questions or have you had enough of this crazy stuff?" Royce's serious face reflected his concern for Jim.

"Yes, I do have another question." Jim cleared his throat.

"Go ahead. I'll try and answer as best I can at this point in the investigation. Remember, so far this is a theory. More work will be done."

"Okay, then. What was the bright light that Mrs. Hadley reported seeing in Mr. Tweeble's house when she called 911?"

Gloria quietly entered the room. In her heart, she didn't want to hear more, but after so many weeks of dealing with the danger, the heartbreak, the fear that smothered her community and upset their lives, she had to get answers to give her hope that the future would not include such atrocities.

"While reviewing eyewitness accounts, including Pamela Gates' information, the state forensics replicated a hot, yellow flash in the lab after studying the make-up of the liquid in the snakes. They combined the liquid with blood containing statins. The chemical reaction created a lot of energy, which is probably what happened when the snakes bit one of the victims. We haven't seen a complete written report yet, only the preliminary information from the experiments."

"So that's what caused the fire on the golf course? The snakes bit one of the golfers who must have been taking statins?" Gloria shuddered, flashing back to the night she watched that scene of panic and death.

"That's what we're assuming right now. But the snakes would have been defending themselves in this situation and not selecting the golfer because he was taking a statin," Royce answered.

Gloria was speechless as she processed all of the information Royce gave them. She glanced at Jim. His face displayed no emotion. Perhaps he was still figuring it all out too.

Gloria sighed. "After all this time of wondering, it's good to know why the snakes preyed upon those unfortunate people."

Gloria walked over to Royce, her hand over her heart. Royce stood up and Gloria embraced him. Finally, the nagging questions about the cause of the deaths of her friends and neighbors answered.

Stepping back, Gloria said, "Thank you for sharing this with us and trusting us with this information. I'm so relieved to know you are making progress in understanding what is going on here. That means you'll have a way to stop these creatures killing spree."

"You're welcome. We feel hopeful we're making progress on a solution."

Gloria's eyes filled with alarm. "Can you imagine what would happen if this becomes public?"

Royce nodded his head. "That's our fear. People who need statins will quit taking them, and their health will be jeopardized. The community is already traumatized by these mutant snakes. Emotionally I don't think they'll be able to handle the truth about the deaths."

"I don't know how you can keep it quiet. That reporter, Heather Blake, is like a bull dog on getting all the facts. She'll find out somehow and go for the exclusive scoop on it. The whole world will know in a few short minutes after she gets done."

Anger surged through her body just thinking about the repercussions of announcing the findings for the cause of the deaths to the public. Heather Blake would be responsible for causing even more tragedy when people stopped taking their medicine.

"That's not something we can discuss right now. That'll be taken care of by another department. We'll have to be vigilant about keeping the records under lock and key, and pray there will be no leaks." Royce said. "Or at least come up with another plausible explanation that will be accepted."

"You mean not exactly telling the whole truth." Jim asked.

Royce didn't face Jim, but instead looked past him when he said, "Well, I didn't actually say that." Royce straightened the papers in his file folder and slid it under his arm holding it tight to his body.

"Are the dogs and King snakes reducing the snake population? Are they having any effect on this war?" Gloria was hopeful, but when she saw Royce's facial expression fall, her heart dropped.

"Well, we can see the results of the K-9 unit kills. We've discovered King snakes with the mutant snakes in their bellies. I'm afraid the worst part of it is we have no way of knowing for sure if we've wiped out this colony. The DEP will monitor the area in years to come and send reports of any sightings to the authorities.

"Snakes have adapted from almost the beginning of time. They were on earth right along with the dinosaurs. Even if a few eggs survive, they can come back to assault us again." Royce stood with his hands clasped together in front of his chest as if in prayer.

Royce's last words startled Gloria. Would the creatures return again? What if they can't be annihilated?

"Hey, I'd better get out of here and let you get some rest," he said.

Jim wrestled himself out of the recliner with some effort. Gloria winced, watching him trying to move those stiff muscles and joints.

When Royce reached the kitchen, he placed his coffee mug on the counter, and turned around to face Jim and Gloria. "You two are pretty special people, and I appreciate your courage to stay here and help us when we needed you."

Royce shook hands with Jim and then focused on Gloria. Instead of offering her hand, she threw her arms around his neck and hugged him even tighter than before. She had no words to tell him how much she appreciated him revealing the truth to them.

After ushering Royce out the kitchen door and saying good-bye, she discovered Jim right behind her. He enfolded her in his arms and she snuggled into his chest. She felt the anxiety and sadness cascade from her shoulders and replaced with peace in her heart.

Gloria closed her eyes relishing this special moment they stood together in their small kitchen. Now, more than ever, she appreciated every minute she and Jim spent together. Circumstances change quickly. Her mother always told her, "The only thing certain in life is change." They couldn't know when one of them would be gone forever.

Jim held her closer and whispered into her hair, "Thank you, Gloria, for being here for me. I love you."

Gloria's voice caught in her throat, but she managed to squeak out, "I love you too, my precious knight in shining armor."

Epilogue

Two years later, Gloria and Jim visited with friends on the deck of the 19th Hole Bar on a lovely, winter evening. The gentle breezes ruffled through the palms. Sand hill cranes awkwardly walked on their thin legs along the fairway. Looking for food, they probed the green grass, completely oblivious of the golfers nearby.

Jim spotted a couple who had recently moved into the community and invited them to sit at the table. Lively conversation, as usual, turned to the topic of the "man-eating snakes."

"Has it been two years already since those snakes were in the neighborhood?" Joe Smith waved his unlit cigar in the air and slugged down another beer. Jim wished Joe hadn't even brought up the subject. Not a good way to welcome newcomers to the community.

"What snakes? I hate snakes." The newcomer frowned at Joe. His bright red nose, cheeks, and his sun-burned bald head were signs he wasn't used to the unforgiving Florida sunshine. "I knew the state had snakes, but I didn't think they were a problem in civilized areas. Otherwise, I wouldn't have bought a home here for the winter."

"Well, there ain't no snakes now after the campaign to get rid of all of 'em after killing…what was it, Gert, a thousand people here?" Joe was obviously exaggerating the story. His beer-enhanced eyes widened as he related the past events. He described Jim's part during the Snake War, so dubbed by the residents of the Citrus Ridge Retirement Community.

Jim Hart had become a legend for killing the deadly snakes with his "golden" shovel. He took a lot of good-natured teasing as well as compliments in his battle against the snakes from hell. Jim would just as soon keep the past buried and never mention it again.

* * *

Deep among the scrub palmetto trees and thick brush, the newborn snakes pushed their way out of the clutch of thirteen eggs laid by the female King snake. These new baby snakes had three brilliant yellow stripes ribboning down their backs. Each one of the hatchlings slithered from the nest, flicking their forked tongues to explore their shrinking habitat.

The End

Please leave
a review.

Help this
Author Catch
More Readers

More BWL Books by J. Q. Rose

http://www.bookswelove.net/authors/rose-j-q/

Deadly Undertaking
Dangerous Sanctuary

Continue reading for an Excerpt of Dangerous Sanctuary

Dangerous Sanctuary

Chapter One

"Wilma, quick! Shut the door! We don't want her escaping from the bedroom." Pastor Christine Hobbs whispered. She pressed her fingers to her lips, signaling Wilma to keep quiet while she surveyed the spacious room.

The bent old lady slammed the wooden door shut with a force that almost knocked it off its hinges. The fugitive was certainly aware of their presence now. The pastor shrugged her shoulders.

"I'm going to check under the bed." Pastor Christine heard the faint ringing of the cell phone in her bag in the living room; however, she was in no position to answer it now. She pulled up the heavy dust ruffle and shined the flashlight under the antique four-poster bed while Wilma wielded the straw broom and waited.

Christine tucked a strand of dark brown hair behind her ear and dived under the bed. As she inched her way along the hardwood floor, dust bunnies and dried bits of food and dirt clung to her black suit coat and slacks. She headed in the direction of the low growling sound.

She had confronted many circumstances not formally taught to young seminarians with stars in their eyes. Today was a prime example. She

170

dared anyone to find a chapter in the textbook detailing guidelines for catching a cat. In the past five years in the pulpit business, she'd faced many realities requiring quick thinking and creativity, and the thirty-two-year-old pastor knew there would be many more in the future.

Christine had promised dear Mrs. Whitcomb she'd find a home for her pet cat, Bitsy, when Mrs. W. went home to be with the Lord. Now she was delivering on her promise, maybe, if she could just catch the dang cat! She and Mrs. Whitcomb's frail sister, Wilma, had chased the speedy creature through several rooms in the old Victorian house, but the nimble black and gray striped cat continued to evade the two women.

This time, she knew she had Bitsy cornered under the bed and hoped she could depend on her partner in the chase to brandish the broom to keep the feisty feline from darting out and away again. What was she thinking? The speed of the old woman could never match the agility of this swift cat.

When the flashlight beamed across the cat's glowing eyes, a cold chill ran down Christine's back. Those eyes were terrifying.

"Okay, Bitsy." She talked softly to the frightened animal. "Please come to me. I'm going to take you home and find someone to take care of you and love you." The growling was much louder. The hairs on the back of Christine's neck stood on end. Would this usually docile cat turn into a tiger and scratch her eyes out? Taking a deep breath, Christine slowly inched forward and offered Bitsy her fingers so she could sniff her hand. "That's a good kitty. You know me from all the times I visited your mistress, don't you?"

Quick as a flash of lightning, Christine grabbed the surprised pet behind her neck and hung on. Growls turned into yowling as she scrambled out from under the bed, dragging the struggling cat, dirt, and dust bunnies with her. She clutched the cat in her arms and scooted back to sit on the floor with her back against the wall, speaking quietly and petting the cat's soft fur to soothe her. After the fierce feline calmed, Christine stood up next to the bed hugging Bitsy to her chest.

"Oh, my. Oh, my," was all Wilma could say when she saw the cat safely in Christine's arms. She unclenched the straw broom and propped it against the wall, then shuffled over to pat the cat's head. "You'll be okay, Bitsy, with Pastor Christine. She'll take good care of you."

"Oh, yes, I will, but only till I can find Bitsy a nice home like I told your sister." Christine smiled at the sweet lady. She freed one hand to brush off the dirt and dust, and now cat hair, on her suit but stopped when Bitsy began struggling to get down.

Christine hurried to retrieve the cat carrier by the kitchen door. Before the cat had a chance to jump away to hide again, she gently shoved the cat into the carrier and latched the door. The yowling cat's protest turned into guttural growls as she settled into the corner of the cage, tail lashing wildly.

"Thanks for your help, Wilma." She stood and faced the eighty-year-old woman who was not exactly adept at catching kitties. Still, she'd offered a lot of moral support.

"Oh, you're welcome. I'll miss her company, but I'm glad to know you'll take good care of her." Wilma's voice choked. "I miss my sister so much. Now I'm all alone."

Christine put her arms around the weeping woman's shoulders and waited for Wilma to compose herself.

"We spent many years together in this house." She pulled a delicate linen handkerchief out of her apron pocket and dabbed her eyes.

Everything would change now for Wilma. She had lost her sister, her pet, her home. She was moving into an assisted living facility at the end of the week. Tomorrow folks from the church would begin packing up everything Wilma wanted to take with her. The remainder of her possessions collected over the sisters' lifetimes would be boxed and donated to the Goodwill. The members volunteered to move her to the facility because there was no family to help Wilma, only the church family. She was counting on all of them to help her settle into her new surroundings.

The pastor hugged the frail woman. "Yes, we'll all miss her." Christine picked up the cat carrier. "Are you okay, Wilma? I can stay with you awhile if you'd like." Christine searched the woman's sad face.

"I'm fine. I'll just get busy packing up a few more boxes. So much to do." Her arms fell to her sides. "You go ahead. I know you have plenty to do too." Wilma smiled and waved her hands to shoo Christine away. "I'm fine."

"Well, I suppose I'd better get Miss Bitsy back to my house and get her situated. I loaded her litter box, bowl, and food in my car. Thanks again for helping me. I'll see you later." She touched Wilma's shoulder. "You get some rest now. God bless you."

* * *

Christine settled the cat in her carrier in the back of her SUV. Bitsy didn't seem so upset now. Hopefully she liked to ride in a car.

She took off for home to drop off the cat and then get back to the church. Having her home in the parsonage across the street from the church was both a blessing and a curse. Close to work, but also available 24 hours a day.

As she approached the house, Christine spotted a police car and ambulance in the church parking lot. She yanked the vehicle's steering wheel so sharply the cat carrier sailed across the back of the car. Her mind raced. *What could be the emergency?* Not taking time to check on the cat, she dashed from her car and sprinted up the steps of the old brown brick church two at a time and raced to the office.

"Oh, Christine, I was just trying to call you again," her secretary, Ella, said.

Christine's face darkened in concern. "Well. I'm glad to see you're okay. What's happened?"

Ella replaced the receiver on the hook. "Dutch found William in the basement. He must have fallen down the steps. We called 9-1-1."

Christine breathed a quick prayer as she rushed down the passing those who had gathered to watch. Ella followed, but it was impossible for her secretary to keep up with Christine's long strides. As she approached the doorway leading to the church basement, a police officer held his palm out to prevent Christine from going downstairs.

"Stop there, ma'am."

"I'm the pastor of this church. I need to see William, our music director. I understand he fell down these stairs." Standing taller, she glared at the officer, challenging him to let her pass.

"I'm sorry, Pastor. No one is allowed down there." He held out his hands to stop her. She tried to discover a way past the officer, but his round body completely blocked the doorway.

She heard Ella and the chorus of church members loudly insist the officer allow the pastor to be with William.

"What's going on up there, Mike?" A gruff voice from the basement yelled up the stairs.

"The pastor wants to come down there, Sir. She is adamant she needs to be with the fallen man."

175

"Send her down."

"Ella would you please get the cat carrier and Bitsy's things from my car and see that she's settled in the parsonage." Christine spoke to her secretary before turning back to the police officer, who shrugged and stepped aside to let her pass. She bounded down the wooden stairs, made the turn on the platform, then gasped as she glimpsed the contorted body of the music director at the bottom of the steps. Her stomach lurched when she saw dried blood from a head wound caked on the floor. She grabbed the railing to steady herself while shifting her gaze away from the nauseating scene. She breathed deeply before looking up again.

Two EMTs stood by doing nothing. Her face flushed with a flash of anger but she guessed there was nothing they could do for a dead man.

The medical examiner investigator motioned her to stop on the flight of stairs. "Sorry, ma'am. Don't come any farther. This is a crime scene. This man is dead."

Chapter Two

Christine's stomach turned over as she grasped the railing once more. Her mind couldn't absorb the reality of William lying dead on the floor of the church basement. *No, he can't be dead!* Her world stopped turning at its usual pace. Instead, everything moved in slow motion as the investigator walked up the basement stairs to meet Christine and escort her up the steps.

"Are you alright?" He helped her turn around on the stairs to return to the hallway, holding her arm as she negotiated the steps. Usually she bounced up these steps, but now she felt like she was trying to climb a mountain.

"I'm okay. I, I need to tell the people waiting in the hallway." She stopped before they got to the platform and faced him. "What happened?"

"I won't know until we investigate the scene and I don't want to speculate. All we know is your music director is definitely dead. I'm sorry." His sad eyes revealed his true feelings while he maintained a professional persona.

"It's my job to tell your folks. I'll do it, but you stay with me, okay?"

"I'm fine. I can do it." She pulled back her shoulders and stood taller.

"Well, ma'am, I know you can do it, but it's my job. They'll need you when I leave, that's for sure."

Christine nodded. They would need her and she would need them to find comfort now and later when trying to deal with the loss of their beloved William.

The group moved to the doorway when Christine and the investigator entered the hallway from the basement.

"I'm so sorry, Pastor, folks. There's nothing you can do for Mr. White now, he's gone and the best you can do is go on home. The police are investigating. The area is sealed off and they'll take care of things. Please, go on home." He held his hands up then dropped them to his side. The graying investigator watched as the group stood silently, waiting until they absorbed the news. Gasps of disbelief rose from the crowd. Some began to cry and hug each other, while a few looked too stunned by the news to react.

Christine clasped her hands tightly together in front of her and took a deep breath to give herself strength her before addressing the gathering of onlookers. "I know it's difficult for us to learn William has passed away. We all have questions, but we need to let the police continue their investigation." Christine's heart shattered as she watched the faces of the members of the congregation distorted by anguish and grief. "Let's meet in the chapel in a few minutes."

She turned to Joanie, the Christian Education Director. "Please go with the group to the chapel and lead them in prayers. I'll join you when I can."

Joanie nodded and invited the bystanders to follow her to the chapel area.

Christine sought a chair in the hallway before her knees buckled. Folding her hands in her lap, she asked God for strength to get through these next few moments. William

White, their music director and her friend was dead. Cold reality stabbed her heart. She tried to contain the pain and nausea building in the pit of her stomach by folding her arms and holding them tight to her body.

What caused William to fall down that flight of stairs and die on the concrete floor of the furnace room? Tears streamed down her face. She had no answers, but she was determined to find out for the sake of his family and her congregation.

* * *

Christine sat next to Dutch, the church's part-time custodian. His giant-sized body dwarfed the folding chair he sat in. He held his face in his large hands and rocked his body back and forth. A white wadded up handkerchief, wet with his tears, lay in his lap.

She rested her hand on his shoulder to let him know of her presence. Detective Cole Stephens sat across from them in the small classroom just across the hall from the large sanctuary. He was part of the team investigating William's death.

"Mr. Van Laan, what time did you discover Mr. White?"

"He's already told the other policemen who were here. Does he have to go through this again? He needs to go home."

"Pastor, I need his story while it's still fresh in his mind. I don't want him to forget the

179

details." He fixed his gaze on Dutch. "When did you find the body, Mr. Van Laan?"

Dutch picked up the handkerchief and wiped his eyes, then loudly blew his nose and looked down at his worn boots. "I came in the church about eight this mornin' and began cleanin' the upstairs bathrooms and pickin' up this and that. I went downstairs to get toilet paper off the storage shelf in the furnace room. I turned on the light at the top of the stairway, and when I turned the corner on the platform halfway down the stairwell, I saw...." Dutch wiped his eyes again and took a deep breath. "I saw William layin' on the floor. I ran down the steps, and there he was all crooked and bloody."

"Did you touch the body?"

"Yes, er no....uh." Dutch's eyes darted to the detective and then to Christine.

She squeezed his shoulder, wondering why the detective wasn't making notes in the notebook in his hand. Why keep questioning Dutch if he wasn't recording the answers? Anger began to build.

Detective Stephens leaned forward in his chair. "Well, what is it? Did you touch him?"

"I'm not sure."

"What do you mean you're not sure? Either you did or didn't." He raised his voice.

"I may have shook him to wake him up." The custodian looked up at Stephens. "I can't remember. I don't know. I can't...I can't..."

"Stop, please. He can't take anymore. You'll have to talk to him later. I'm taking him home now." Christine's eyes blazed as she faced the detective.

She stood up. He looked at her with a smug smile. "Yeah, go ahead and take him home, but you may want to clean up a bit, Pastor. By the way, how did you get that dirty?" His brown eyes twinkled as he scanned her from head to toe.

She looked at the front of her jacket and pants and remembered the dust and food particles still clinging to her clothes. She ignored the detective and went to Dutch. "Come on, Dutch. I'll take you home."

Detective Stephens stood up but did nothing to stop them from leaving.

He called after her, "I'll be back to interview you and the secretary and anyone who was here this morning when the body was found."

Chapter Three

Thank goodness for garage door openers. Christine cut the SUV into the driveway of the parsonage as she noted the news media gathered in the church parking lot. She hit the accelerator and escaped into the garage the minute the door opened.

She rested her forehead on the wheel while the door closed behind her and allowed the silence to engulf her before facing the chaos. She just wanted the long day to end. William's death, Dutch coping with the questions from the police, counseling his family, upset parishioners calling.

Christine grabbed her bag and briefcase off the passenger side floor, and made her way through the garage. When she opened the door leading into the kitchen, a dark shadow disappeared into the dining room. She jumped at the quick movement and then smiled when she realized it had to be Bitsy.

"Here, Bitsy. Here, kitty."

Walking into the house owned by the church and maintained by the parsonage committee was like re-visiting the '70's era. The interior of the house was decorated, if that's what you'd call it, in avocado green and harvest gold. The harvest gold kitchen appliances functioned well thanks to regular maintenance by a church member who was a retired electrician.

Christine dropped her bag and keys on the kitchen counter and called the frightened cat. From the presence of the full bowls of water and food on the kitchen floor, she knew Ella had taken care of Bitsy. Even the litter box was filled and ready. She imagined her kind secretary stayed awhile and comforted Bitsy, too.

"Here, kitty, kitty, kitty. Here, Bitsy."

The doorbell buzzed. She wanted to ignore the clamoring reporters outside on the front porch but knew they would only hound her until she talked to them. Opening the door to a sea of cameras and people shouting questions, she motioned to the group for silence and then announced, "I have no comment at this time." She heard protests and more questions as she shut the steel door, locked it, and slid the security bolt in place.

Setting her briefcase on the floor beside her chair, Christine plopped down in her one recliner in the living room.

Bitsy peeked out from behind the couch. Scooting to the front of the chair, she bent down and motioned to the cat. "Come on, kitty. Come on over here, Bitsy."

The cat warily approached. "Here, kitty, kitty, kitty." Just as she sat back in the recliner, the cat leapt onto her lap. Christine ran her hand from the top of the cat's head, along her spine, all the way across the fluffy tail. Bitsy arched her back and purred. Kneading her front paws into Christine's legs, her purring grew louder and louder.

As Bitsy settled on her lap, Christine loosened her tight muscles and gazed around her sparsely furnished living room. The neutral landlord-white wall color a sterile background for the heavy green and gold draperies at the picture windows in the front of the house.

But she felt at home with the over-sized lamp on the end table near the recliner, a few folding chairs from the church, and an old couch which fit right into the parsonage's '70's décor. A gray card table and chairs served as a temporary dining table in the dining room just off the kitchen and living room.

Her bedroom upstairs contained the handsome dark cherry bedroom suite, remnants of her marriage to Brad. They were the only items she had fought for after their divorce two years ago.

She smiled as she looked into the cat's face and continued petting its smooth, silky coat. In a sense, assuming the care of this pet would be one of her more pleasant duties as church pastor. This career took most of her time. Even after nine months, she hadn't made time to furnish her home. Instead, she'd concentrated on being the spiritual leader of the three hundred souls at Dayspring Church in Fair Lake, Michigan.

Christine closed her eyes for a minute and then quickly opened them to dispel the vision of

William sprawled on the basement floor. How would she ever erase that image from her mind? She rubbed her eyes in an attempt to ward off a dull headache forming behind her eyes.

Her thoughts turned to Dutch, the sweet man who entertained the Sunday School kids, helped out with church dinners, and took pride in making the church shine. After the detective interviewed him in the Sunday school room, Christine spent several hours with the distraught man and his family at their home. His wife, Kendra, and their two grown children were outraged that the police suspected their husband and father of murder.

In her mind, Christine began to construct the words she would need to notify William's sister of his death. Even with her years of experience behind her, it was never easy to tell a family member or friend their loved one was dead.

Hi sister Claire lived an hour away, and Christine hoped she hadn't already heard about his accident on the news. As far as she knew Claire and her husband were William's only family. He had never talked about an ex-wife or a girlfriend. Christine's brow crinkled when she considered that after nine months of working with William at the church, she really didn't know much about him, as he'd never spoken about his personal life.

She grinned when she remembered his tousled thick brown hair, warm eyes, and deep laughter echoing throughout the church hallways. Christine pictured him dressed in one of his famous T-shirts. He had a reputation for his T-shirt collection. Every time she saw him, he wore a different colorful shirt graced with clever, humorous sayings and graphics.

Christine and William shared a love of music. For the thirteen years of his tenure as music director at Dayspring Church he'd proven himself an accomplished musician. His performances on the organ filled the hearts of the congregation with awe and wonder and as choir director he'd taught the choir members to mesh their voices beautifully and bring the presence of God into the sanctuary.

He considered the members of the children's choir "his" kids, and shared their excitement whether they were playing a sport, performing in a play, or winning a science award. He'd been well known and loved in the community from his participation in service groups outside of the church. Christine's eyes teared up. She would miss him and his lively spirit.

Christine jumped when the doorbell buzzed, followed by a loud, "Yoo-hoo!" The cat hopped off her lap, and Christine climbed out of the recliner. She rushed to unlock and open the kitchen door. Lacey marched in with a bouquet of flowers and a brown paper bag.

"Hey, Chris. How ya' doin'?" Lacey placed the vase of red and yellow tulips on the kitchen counter and walked toward Christine. "I heard about William. I'm so sorry." Lacey wrapped her arms around Christine and hugged hard.

The tall pastor and the petite florist couldn't have been more different in appearance. Lacey's blunt cut strawberry blonde hair and bright floral shirt and jeans contrasted with the minister's black suit and shoulder length brown hair. Because they were so alike in their life experiences, they'd become fast friends. They were nearly the same age, both single, both uncommitted, and both had marriages that had ended badly.

Lacey held out the brown bag. "Here, I brought us some light beers. I figured you needed some company." She smiled big, reminding Christine how much she loved her friend.

"You're so thoughtful. Thanks for the beer and the beautiful flowers."

"Aw, you're welcome." Lacey waved off the comment and moved toward Bitsy.

"What a sweet kitty. Is this Mrs. Whitcomb's cat? She's beautiful." Lacey bent down to pat the now friendly feline.

"Yeah, that's Bitsy. She wasn't interested in coming home with me." Christine watched as her friend easily stroked the cat. "You certainly have a way with cats. It took me quite awhile before Bitsy would even look at me. Have a seat."

Each grabbed a beer and twisted off the caps as they settled themselves on the big ugly couch for a warm heart-to-heart talk. Bitsy chose to stretch out on the back of the couch lounging between the two women. For a few minutes, the pastor relaxed and allowed herself to forget her responsibilities and just enjoyed having a friend. Lacey helped to fill the void Christine had felt after divorcing Brad, whom she thought would be her soul mate forever.

"I heard Cole Stephens is the investigator on William's case," said Lacey. "He's gorgeous." She grinned a silly face at Christine and then sucked down more beer.

"You've got to be kidding me. I was so worried about Dutch, I didn't even notice."

"Well, I'm sure you had your mind on a lot more than Cole Stephens. Take my word for it, he's a cutie." Lacey winked.

Christine tried to picture Cole Stephens. He was a tall, muscular man and handsome in his tie and sport coat. She remembered his short-cropped hair. Was it a flattop, or was there some spiky hair sticking out? Did he wear glasses or not? Her memory of him was too fuzzy.

"I didn't exactly have my man radar out this morning." She tried to brush off more of the cat hair, dust, and food particles on her suit coat and slacks.

"Well, I'm sure he'll be talking to you some more if this investigation turns up foul play."

Christine sat straight up on the couch and faced her friend. "Why would you even say something like that? You know William probably just tripped down the steps. Gosh, Lacey. What a thing to say!"

"I'm just sayin'…just wondering…I mean, really, Chris, nobody knows anything about William. He may have had too much wine and fell down the steps, or maybe he discovered a burglar in the church, or any of a dozen things. Just sayin'…" Lacey quickly took another swig of the cold beer.

Focusing intently on Christine's eyes, she said, "Cole Stephens has a reputation for digging for the truth. He won't settle for any old explanation of William's death. You have to be prepared for the worst."

The End

If you enjoyed this book, please leave a review.

In eBook and print from JQ Rose

Deadly Undertaking
Dangerous Sanctuary

J Q Rose is an avid reader, photographer, and blogger with blogs about writing and growing a vegetable garden. Janet and her husband are snow birds who spend winters in Florida, allowing them to garden twelve months out of the year. Summer finds her up north camping and hunting toads, frogs, and salamanders with her grandchildren.